Rooted

Marjorie Ditolla

Bladensburg, Maryland

Dove Christian
Publishers

A Division of Kingdom Christian Enterprises
PO Box 611
Bladensburg, MD 20710-0611

ISBN 978-1-957497-46-4

Published in the United States of America

Contents

Preface vii

Mamma 1

Early Memories 9

Mamma's Sickness 19

A New Home For The Boys 24

Doris's Promise 35

Moving – Almost Together 43

Settling In 56

A New School 67

A New Job 72

A Big Sister For A Big Sister 82

Good Morning Good Afternoon 93

The Good, The Bad And The Wrinkled 104

Nurse Doris 118

Together Alone 125

Oscar's Birthday Party With Pappa 134

Quarantined 151

Back to "Normal" 161

Exploring Out Back 169

West Park 178

Real Live Country 187

The Creek 199

A Friend for Doris 213

Nine Years Old 220

Preface

 once found myself trying to help my almost four-year-old grandnephew understand that his grandmother was my sister, and Gram was our mother. Despite every attempt, the confused child just stared blankly, before deciding it was time to move on to a different game. His five and a half year old sister, had no problem with the concept, and actually seemed to enjoy gaining an understanding of the relationships.

I don't remember a specific moment I fully understood that my mother's life didn't begin when she became my mother. But when my own children had grown and were off on their own and circumstances gave my husband and me the privilege of living near my mother, we had time to deepen our relationship. I began to pull together some of the pieces of her life, and truly appreciate the beauty and foundation of who she is.

While I sat opposite her in her living room, Mom related stories of her youth. Some were familiar, but many were new. I had seen where she lived as a child, but as I listened, the stories she related made the people and places come alive. I began to feel like I was there, watching the Haukland children going through their childhood experiences.

In the dim light next to her reclining chair, while she was replacing the elastic on an old pair of her slacks, we laughed together as we recalled the many times she would mend or darn our clothing, give it back to us and say, "Just wear it one more time." That meant it was back in circulation, and we were expected to wear it, until it needed additional repairs.

When my sisters and I were kids, I guess we thought Mom's frugal ways were all about our family. Our father was a police officer with a modest income, and he would work as a handyman for the neighbors, to make extra money. Mom, who was a registered nurse, stayed home with us, so there was no income from her. Mom sewed a lot of our clothes, and we had some very nice hand-me-downs from the girls who lived up the street. Even though they were more expensive clothes, they had already been through two girls when we got them, and we kind of felt sorry for ourselves that we didn't have new clothes like our friends. Nevertheless, Mom kept our clothes washed and any holes or open seams were quickly mended.

Mom was a very hard worker, and she had a positive, happy attitude and a gentle, quiet spirit. Her mother had introduced our mother to God in her very early years, in stories and songs, and her relationship with God grew, as she did.

While we were growing up, it was rare to find our mom sitting down. But there was one very special time, before the sun rose in the morning; Mom would be sitting in the wingback chair in the living room. It was the time between when our father left for work and we got up for school. We would sneak down the stairs to see her, but it was like catching Santa filling stockings; we loved to find her there, but we knew that she should not be disturbed. This was the foundation for Mommy's day. She would read her Bible, then with her Bible closed in her lap, her hands folded and peacefully resting on it, Mom would be talking to her Heavenly Father.

The more I think about Mom's life, the more I appreciate the depth of her spirit, and I understand why she made the very best use of everything she had, and with a grateful attitude. When we gave her an old chair, or a book or a ball of wool, she would find a niche for the chair, read the book and make something special with the wool.

Realizing some of the things she faced were very difficult, I sometimes asked, "How did you feel about that?" She would say in a very matter of fact way: "That's just the way it was."

It became clear that Mom's frugal ways, along with so many other patterns we saw and came to respect in her life, didn't begin with her children. These were deeply ingrained in Mom from her childhood: wisdom to adjust her attitude when circumstances couldn't be changed, to accept what she had and make the best of it, and her faith - taking God at his word, and living without restrictions, trusting in His love and provisions.

In her honor, and to honor Our Heavenly Father, I have taken liberty to tell, in story form, what I understand of her early years. Some names may be fictitious or changed for privacy.

It is my hope and prayer that those who come behind her, both as her descendants and those in situations who identify with what my mother has grown through, will be blessed by learning how, out of loss and little, grew a deeply rooted, truly beautiful person.

Colossians 2:6 and 7

Chapter 1
Mamma

In February 1912, just two months before the Titanic in all its splendor, sank on its maiden voyage across the Atlantic Ocean, a young Norwegian woman, traveling by herself, boarded a less glamorous ship, the SS United States, to make her way to America.

S.S. United States

"Aagot Ostberg?"

"Ja."

The bursar put a check by her name (number twenty

eight) on the passenger list, and confirmed where she was to stay during the trip.

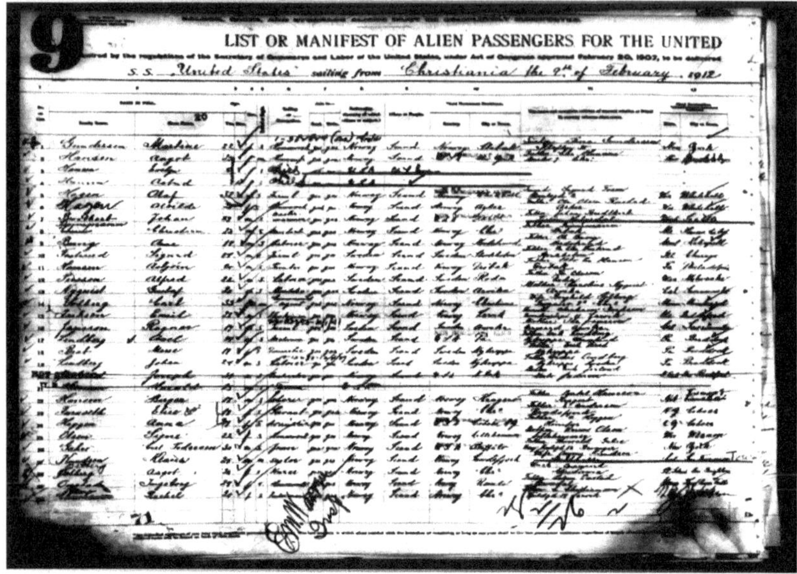

List of Passengers

She gave one last hug to her Uncle Oppregard, who had brought her to the ship, then turned, and overcoming the fear that was trying to keep her from boarding, boldly made the lonely, frightening ascent up the plank, beginning the journey to her new life in America. Aagot stood by herself at the rail on the upper deck, between two couples who were standing arm in arm, waving to friends and family who had brought them to the ship. She watched the porters load her trunk. This cumbersome chest contained all the possessions she would ever have to remind her of the life she was leaving. She had carefully selected pictures, clothing, blankets, a few small dishes and a few hardanger doilies and ornaments from her home in Christiansen, Norway. Taking in a deep breath, she mustered what she hoped would look like an enthusiastic smile and waved goodbye to her uncle.

Mamma

As the ship was pulling out of its berth, Aagot tried to glimpse past the dock and take in what might well be her last look at her homeland. Norway became a smaller and smaller speck until it was no longer visible.

Aagot squared her shoulders and reminded herself that she was a 26-year-old woman, and she was ready for this huge step. Though her language was Norwegian, she was fluent in both writing and speaking English. She had completed her training as a nurse, and besides, she would have family where she was going. Her brother Bjarne and his wife, Jessie and her sister Ulla and her sister's husband, Oscar were already settled in America. Her sister and brother-in-law would be there to meet her when she arrived in twelve days.

The days and nights seemed long, and the accommodations were crowded. Many of the passengers became sea sick and spent most of the time in their bunks, but Aagot spent as much time as she could on the ships deck. There was nothing to see but water, sky, and other passengers from the deck. Her clothes whipped around in the wind and the salty air was cold against her face, yet Aagot wanted to impress every moment of her trip into her memory.

As each day passed, she tried to imagine what this new world would look like, and how Ulla and Oscar would look as they greeted her in New York. She wondered if the people she met would speak English so quickly, that she would have trouble understanding them, and what if she hadn't learned the English words for some of the medical terms she might be expected to know.

Finally, on February 21, 1912, with its loud horn sounding, the SS United States entered New York Harbor. Tugboats met the ship, and the usually crowded deck was now so full that it was hard for Aagot to keep her feet anchored to the deck. The passengers were all straining to see the Statue of Liberty, America's gift from France that was the symbol of being welcomed into America. As they entered the harbor, everyone seemed to point ahead and to the left, where the statue was seen holding the torch high above her head. It was cold, but sunny, and Aagot felt an overwhelming sense of joy and expectation, as their ship was guided past the Statue of Liberty to Ellis Island.

Many immigrants began life in America, at Ellis Island, where friends or family met them. Every unmarried woman had to have a sponsor, who accepted responsibility for helping her get settled and be assimilated into the country. Ulla, Aagot's younger sister, would be Aagot's sponsor.

The ship arrived a day before schedule, so once they disembarked, most of the passengers were scurrying to contact their relatives. Ulla and Oscar had no phone. They had made all of the arrangements by mail, so Aagot would have to settle herself somewhere out of the way, in the main building, and wait. There were others who had to wait, but most of them were released before nightfall.

The big stone building was cold and noisy during the day and at night. Whenever a ship arrived, the passengers formed lines waiting to complete the necessary paperwork and be examined by doctors.

Aagot settled herself against the wall, next to a heater, where she watched as most of those she had seen many times on their trip left the island to begin their adventures. The only immigrants who had accommodations to stay in this building were those who were detained for sickness. They were kept in an isolated area and monitored by physicians to be certain they were not bringing contagious illnesses into the country.

Aagot opened her trunk and although she was reluctant to use her precious possessions on the dirty floor of the Immigration Building, she was glad to have an afghan her mother had knit and another lusekofte sweater to put on, to keep her warm. Klara and her son (two of the remaining passengers) joined Aagot on the floor near the heater.

Aagot's sister and brother-in-law arrived late the next morning. Once the papers were signed, they left at 11:25. Aagot, Ulla and Oscar wrestled with the big, heavy trunk as they made their way onto and off a ferry, a train, another ferry then a bus, to get to her sister's flat, on Staten Island, New York.

What a relief to finally have reached her destination. Aagot and Ulla stayed up talking most of the night, catching up on the things that couldn't be shared in a letter. They decided Aagot would stay with her sister while she looked for a job and completed all the paperwork she would need to work as a nurse in America. Aagot enjoyed cooking, and Ulla and Oscar were happy to come home after work to a hot, Norwegian meal. On the weekends, she would go with her sister and brother-in-law to a club in Brooklyn, called The Sons of Norway. Norwegian emigrants came from all over Brooklyn, Staten Island, even as far as New Jersey, to get together. There was music, food and dancing just like there was in Norway, and the only language everyone spoke while they were there, was Norwegian.

Before long, Aagot met a young man who had come to America from Norway seven years earlier. He came on a work visa, and once he had completed the work in Louisiana, he moved north, into the large Norwegian community in New York. In Norway, when a family works on a farm, they take its owner's last name. His last name was Haukland. His full name was Magnus Peder Petersen Haukland. Once he left Norway, he never worked as a farmer. He had many different jobs, on or near the water. When Aagot met Magnus, he worked for a company in Brooklyn that repaired ships and stored ships on dry land when they weren't being used. The company had many employees, and Magnus worked on a tugboat in New York Harbor.

On December 21, 1912, they were married. Aagot and Magnus rented a flat in Brooklyn, near the pier the tugboat Magnus worked on, was docked.

Their first child was born with a very serious problem in the development of his spine, and he died when he was just a few months old.

By the end of July 1914, Aagot and Magnus were expecting another baby. One hot summer morning, in the middle of July, Magnus asked Aagot if she'd like to spend the day relaxing on the tugboat while he was working. Comfortable that she still had a few weeks until the baby was due to arrive, Aagot decided to accept her husband's invitation. Their flat was so hot during the day, and on the water, it would be breezy and cool. She could sit on the deck and relax while the sailors worked.

Aagot appreciated the chance to be out on the water. She had been a little uncomfortable, but that was expected. Soon, however, she realized that what she thought was a passing discomfort, was progressing in intensity to being in labor. Her new baby would be born before there was time or a way that she could get to a hospital.

While her husband and the other sailors were busy at work, Aagot found a quiet place inside the cabin of the boat, and told the men not to disturb her. She remained calm, and between contractions, she prepared as much as she could, for the delivery of her baby. She boiled water and sterilized the only knife she could find, to cut the umbilical cord. She spread a clean blanket on the berth. Her labor was strong but quick, and before the sailors delivered the ship to its berth, Aagot safely gave birth to her baby.

Although the baby was actually born on a tugboat in the Verrazano Narrows, her birth certificate says she was born on Staten Island, on the 17th day of July 1914. After a day of hard labor for both parents, Aagot and Magnus brought their beautiful, healthy, blue-eyed, red-haired daughter, whom they named Dorris Margareth, home. Aagot now stayed at home and cared for her baby.

Aagot and Dorris

Twenty months later, Dorris got a sister, Christina Ulleraikke.

Magnus, Aagot, Dorris and Christina

Oscar Philip came twenty-two months after Christina.

Chapter 2
Early Memories

*O*n a warm spring afternoon, Aagot had been sitting on the step discreetly nursing Oscar and watching Dorris push Christina in her carriage.

"Dorris, I have to go inside and change Oscar's diaper. You stay out here with Christina."

"O. K., Mamma"

When Christina fell asleep in the carriage, Dorris had no one to play with. She parked the carriage near their door and went in the house to see what Mamma was doing, forgetting that she was babysitting for Christina. When Mamma realized Christina was outside alone, she ran to check on her, but the carriage with the baby in it, was gone.

Aagot screamed with fear, and ran with Oscar in her arms, from one end of the street to the other looking for her baby daughter. Dorris ran behind her, holding the back of her mother's shirt and crying, but not sure exactly why.

Pappa happened to be walking home from work when he spotted the well-worn baby carriage with the bright yellow bow on the hood. A woman he did not know was pushing it away from their street; but he was so certain it was his carriage that he called out to the woman, "STOP! STOP! That's my baby!"

When the woman who had been pushing the carriage began to run with it, Magnus's suspicion was confirmed. The woman continued to run, pushing the carriage, but when Magnus began to catch up to her, she abandoned the carriage and continued to run from him.

Instead of continuing to follow her, Magnus picked up Christina who had been awakened by the reckless movement and was crying. Holding her in one arm, he pushed their old carriage with the other hand and rushed home.

Mamma was so happy to see her daughter. When Christina stopped crying, and Magnus caught his breath after running, he explained what had happened. Dorris who was only four years old, did not realize what she had done wrong at first, but this experience imprinted a strong sense of responsibility for her siblings that would only grow stronger with time.

The small Brooklyn flat that was so comfortable when Aagot and Magnus had first gotten married was far too small for their current family of three with a fourth baby on the way. They found a larger ground floor flat, in Elizabeth, NJ, just down the street from where Aagot's brother, Bjarne and his wife Jessie lived.

When Oscar was twenty-one months old, Alerth Moogans Haukland was born. Now there were four children, two girls and two boys. Dorris was six, Christina four, Oscar was almost two, and Alerth was the newborn baby.

The street they lived on was lined on both sides with two story houses that all looked exactly the same. Most of them were attached to each other on both sides, but there was a space between some of them that was just wide enough for someone to walk through to get into the back yard, that they all shared. Each house had one front door on the outside, but inside, there was a door to the flat on the first floor and a flight of stairs up to the flat on the second floor. There was also a flight of steps that went down to the basement where coal was stored. It was dark and scary down there. A flat was different from an apartment because it didn't have built-in heat or hot water.

The Haukland's flat had a dining room, living room, and a kitchen. The entrance to their flat was in the dining room, which had a modest table, five chairs and a high chair. In the winter, the dining room was quite cold because the only heat in this room came from the other rooms. In the living room there was a sofa, a chair, two beds and a crib. One bed was for the parents and one for the children. The girls slept at one end and Oscar slept at the other end. The baby slept in the crib. In the winter, a small kerosene stove heated the living room. It sat on the floor, and could be moved around the room, depending on where they needed the heat.

On the right side of the kitchen, there was the big, black cast iron stove that was fueled by either wood or coal. In the winter, it was always kept warm, because it served as a heater as well as a stove and oven. In the summer, it was used as little as possible, because it would make the flat even hotter. After the stove, was the sink, then a short counter by the window looking out at the back yards. This window opened widely, and gave access to a clothes line that was one of many that were attached by a pulley to a tall, fat pole in the yard. This is where laundry would be hung to dry.

Rooted

On the left side, upon entering the kitchen, there was a small, painted, wooden, closet with a little metal latch on the door. It wasn't really a bathroom, because there was no tub or shower or sink, but in the closet there was a toilet. Hanging high on the wall behind the toilet was a large wooden box. A pipe brought water to fill the box and when the long chain that hung from the box was pulled, it would let water from the box flow into the toilet, to flush it. Baths were taken by heating water on the stove and filling a basin to wash from.

Laundry was done in the sink. The clothes were soaked then rubbed up and down against a rippled piece of metal in a wooden frame that was placed in the sink so the water from the clothes would run back into the sink.

After it was washed, it would be rinsed, twisted and squeezed to take out most of the water, then hung out on the line in the yard, to dry. The children were happy and enjoyed playing with each other. The girls enjoyed having a real baby for a doll, and Oscar kept busy playing with a ball, or trying to fit into the girl's play. Aagot was very busy, day and night caring for her young family. As she worked, she often sang to her children and taught them many songs in both English and Norwegian. She also told and read stories to them, mostly from the Bible.

Aagot's mother had been an accomplished pianist, and Aagot also had a special gift for music. One of the neighbors would pay Aagot to tune her piano, and she invited Aagot to bring her children and play the piano for them. Singing with the piano was even more fun than when it was just their voices.

Caring for her home and four young children was a challenge when they were all healthy, but the children often became sick with childhood diseases, most of which have become very rare since vaccinations were invented. When one child became sick, in a few days the next one also became sick, then the next and then the next. Usually the older ones became sick first, and by the time the younger children became sick, the older ones were just about over the sickness, and they could help their mother care for and entertain the babies.

Because she was a nurse, Aagot cared especially well for her children. Sometimes she hung sheets around the sickest children's bed, to quarantine them. Dorris would use the sheets that were hanging from the ceiling, as a curtain for her make-believe stage. She would put on a show for the sick children, singing and dancing, or she would make a puppet show with socks that she put over her hands and up her arms. This helped the children who were itchy or cranky to forget about their discomfort for a while, and she even got them to laugh. Their mother appreciated the distraction for the sick children, and took that time to catch up on her work, or take a much-needed nap.

During the summer, when their flat got very hot, the children loved to go outside and play. Aagot would sit on the step while the children played on the sidewalk between the house and the street. There wasn't much traffic on their street, and most of the vehicles were horse-drawn carts making deliveries to the stores down the street from them. The sidewalk was narrow, but the four small children managed to play there for hours.

When the big horse-pulled water tank went through the street spraying water to clean the cobble stones and wash off the manure that was left there by the horses, the Hauklands were allowed to jump and splash in the puddles that formed on the side of the street. That was their relief from the heat, and the most water available for them to play in.

One day, as they were playing in front of the house, a man with a donkey cart was riding down their street, calling out, "Pictures - I take pictures!"

Aagot waved the man over, and told her children to sit on the step that was the entrance to their flat. She ran inside and dug money from the cookie jar to pay the photographer.

Once Dorris entered school, Mamma decided the Children should use more common American spelling of their names. Dorris became Doris, Christina became Christine, Oscar remained the same and Alerth became Alert.[1]

---

1 Alert is pronounced like Albert but without the b sound.

Doris loved school, and loved playing school with her sister and brothers when she got home. She also loved sitting with her mother in the evenings and she learned how to sew and knit.

Even though she was young to run errands outside their home, sometimes her mother had no choice, but to ask Doris to take her sister and go to the grocery store.

"What can I do for you two young ladies?" the grocer asked.

"My mother wants a quart of milk and a loaf of bread," Doris answered in the most grown up voice she had.

"Is that all?"

"No," added Christine, "a bag of sugar, too."

"Christine," Doris whispered as the grocer walked to the back of the store. "Mamma doesn't want us to buy sugar!"

But Christine was very strong-willed, and Doris lacked sufficient authority and was too pre-occupied with her own task, to change Christine's mind, so they left for home with milk, bread and sugar.

"Christine, that sugar cost a lot of money, and Mamma didn't want us to buy sugar, today!" Doris said loud and clearly after they left the store. Then, being afraid to arrive home with the bag of sugar, Christine bit a hole in the bag, and let the sugar pour out as she walked. She could still taste that first mouthful of sugar when the trail stopped because the bag was empty. Then she threw the bag into a trashcan on the street.

Another time, when both boys were sick, and their father was not home, Doris and Christine were sent to buy coal. Doris knew the way, as she had gone to the coal yard with each of her parents before. She was confident that she could handle this very important errand.

On the way, Christine noticed a hole in the little wooden bridge they had to cross. The hole was not even big enough for her to fit her foot into, but she would not take another step. She said, "NO, I won't walk on the bridge." Knowing that the errand was important and it was she who had to solve the problem, Doris carried her sister across the bridge to the coal yard. Coming home, she walked across the bridge twice - first with the coal, and then she went back and carried her sister until they were on solid ground.

The company Magnus worked for had grown very busy and important. This was because the United States used this company to work on the ships it needed for the World War. But after the war was over, they didn't have as much work for their employees. Magnus wasn't able to find another job or get more work at his company. It became necessary for Aagot to return to work as a nurse, so they would have enough money for the rent and to buy food and clothes.

Doris was now in first grade. Although she was still young, she was very responsible and able to significantly help in caring for the other children and their home. By now, she was able to knit and could help her mother with the sewing and darning. Doris was almost completely independent in caring for herself, and she loved helping her mother in any way she could.

In the mornings, Aagot would get herself ready for work, and with Doris's help, get Christine ready for school and the boys ready to go to the nursery. Doris brought the youngest two to the nursery on her way to school and Aagot walked Christine to kindergarten. Then she walked to the nursing home where she worked. After a half day at school, Christine would stay at Aagot's brother, Uncle Bjarnes's house to be watched by Aunt Jessie until Aagot finished work for the day.

At three fifteen, after school, Doris, would come to the nursing home to wait for her mother's shift to end. As she got more comfortable with the patients there, she would put on shows for them. Doris loved to sing and dance, and here she was the star! The patients looked forward to the entertainment she provided. She was a happy child with soft skin and curly red hair. In their craft time, they would make big bows for her hair.

On the way home, Doris would just about burst with enthusiasm telling her mother about her day at school. After they gathered the boys from the nursery and her sister from Uncle Bjarne's house, they'd go home and prepare dinner together, then wait for Pappa to come home.

One night, it got too late to wait for Pappa. After all the children including Doris, were asleep, there was a loud knock at the door. Doris woke up with the noise, but was afraid to show that she was awake. She lay still in her bed, and heard her mother answer the door. It sounded like two Norwegian men were there with her father. The men asked Aagot if they could help her with her husband, and she answered in Norwegian, "No, thank you, I can take him from here." Doris's father seemed to be having trouble walking, and her mother was directing him toward the kitchen.

Before she fell back to sleep, Doris heard her father speaking loudly, and her mother trying to quietly answer him. It sounded like her mother was crying. The next morning, neither Doris nor her mother spoke about this. Magnus stayed in bed, and was still asleep when they left the house to deliver the young children where they belonged and then go to work and school, as usual.

A month later, on a cold winter evening, Doris and her Mamma had dinner all ready. The house was nice and warm and Christine and Oscar were playing together while they were waiting for Pappa. Aagot was sitting in the living room nursing Alert. Tired from being on her feet at work all day, she said, "Doris, would you please bring the baby's carriage to me?" She quickly reconsidered her request, realizing the possibility that in getting the large carriage past the stove, which was in the middle of the room, the little girl might knock over the portable kerosene stove and start a fire. Aagot quickly said, "No - don't do it! You might knock the stove over," but it was too late.

Confident that she could do it well enough to please her mother, and so eager to help, she continued toward her mother, saying, "I can do it Mamma, I'll be careful." Doris peered around the side of the carriage nearest the stove, and began to inch past it. As her Mamma had predicted, with the gentlest nudge, the stove toppled over. The kerosene poured out and fire quickly spread through the room.

Aagot got all the children out safely, then, since they had no telephone, she ran down the street with the baby in her arms, yelling, "Fire, Fire," in her strong Norwegian accent. By the time the fire department arrived, the flat was damaged to the extent that the family could no longer live there.

With no help from friends or family, they salvaged what they could, and moved into another first floor flat on the same street. There they resumed their efforts to make a better life for themselves and their children. They were in their new flat for less than a year, when Aagot became ill, and was hospitalized.

Chapter 3
Mamma's Sickness

While their mother was in the hospital, Doris and Christine were brought to Uncle Bjarne's house, so they could continue going to school, and the babies, Oscar and Alert went to Aagot's sister, Tante[2] Ulla's house, which was now also in Elizabeth, New Jersey. Aagot was expected to be home in a few days, but after she had been in the hospital for several weeks, things did not look promising. When Magnus came to Uncle Bjarne's house one evening, he greeted his little girls, then sat at the dining room table with Uncle Bjarne, as usual.

Doris and Christine returned to playing with their dolls in the living room. As they played, Doris thought she heard her father crying. She didn't say anything to Christine, and tried hard to continue playing so Christine wouldn't hear him crying and run into the dining room to see for herself. This made Doris feel kind of grown-up. She often had to creatively direct Christine, without her being aware of what Doris was doing. In addition to being younger, Christine was used to asserting herself to get her way or at least have some say, in most situations.

2 Tante is Norwegian for *Aunt*

From the living room, Doris could see Aunt Jessie standing, with her dishtowel draped over her shoulder, behind their father. Her hand was resting on his back. In a little while, the crying stopped, and Magnus came into the living room. His eyes were definitely red, Doris noted to herself, but she said nothing.

In as much of an ordinary voice as he could, Magnus called Doris to his side as he sat in one of the big soft chairs. Christine continued to play, so he was able to talk with Doris, quietly without her interfering. "Doris," he said, swallowing hard, "Mamma is still very sick. She asked me to bring you to the hospital to see her."

Although her Pappa crying was very unusual, Doris could not understand how serious this visit would be. She again felt very grown-up, and actually felt happy and excited at the thought of seeing her mother. She truly missed being with her mother, and she longed to return to the routines they were used to.

The hospital was warm, and had a strange smell, like the place where Mamma worked. Everything was white there, the walls, the floors, the doors, the worker's clothing. Unlike Mamma's work, there were no people sitting in the halls, in their wheel chairs.

Pappa held her hand as they walked down the hall. Doris looked into the rooms they were passing, and she could see people in their beds. Some waved to her, some were making groaning noises, and some were being taken care of by nurses. Pappa paused suddenly and squatted down to speak softly to his grown-up little girl. "Doris, this is Mamma's room," he said, pointing to the next room they would come to. "Mamma is very tired from being sick, and she doesn't speak as loudly as usual, but she wanted to see you, and to talk to you, anyway. Try hard to listen to her."

Mamma's Sickness

There were no words that could have prepared Doris for what she saw. Except for her long, dark brown hair that was all stringy and needed to be brushed, Mamma was as white as the sheets she was lying in. When they entered the room, Mamma didn't even open her eyes. Pappa touched her hand gently and leaned over by her ear and said, "Aagot, Doris is here to see you."

"Doris," she said in a very low voice with her eyes still closed. "Doris!" she said again in a little louder voice, opening her eyes. Using every bit of strength she had, Aagot lifted her head and shoulders off the bed, and leaned toward her precious child until their eyes met. With her pale, cracked lips, Aagot formed a faint smile and said, "Doris, please keep the family together."

With that, she slumped back onto her pillow, and her eyes closed again. "Pappa!" Doris cried, "Is Mamma all right?"

Pappa was staring at Mamma's face. It was different. He was seeing a peace that replaced the restless, distressed look he had seen as he sat beside her and held her hand for the last few weeks.

Pappa reassured Doris, "Mamma is just going to go back to sleep now. Give her a kiss, and we'll go back to Christine, and let Mamma get some more rest."

Doris stood on her toes and gladly kissed her mother's cheek, but Mamma didn't seem to know that she had kissed her. Doris didn't remember Mamma ever being so tired that she didn't wrap her arms around her and kiss her back. Doris didn't understand this. She just knew that Mamma wasn't coming home, yet, and it probably would be a long time until things would be back to normal.

That was the last time Doris saw her mother alive.

No one ever went home again except Pappa. The boys stayed with Aagot's sister, Tante Ulla and Christine and Doris stayed with Uncle Bjarne and Aunt Jessie.

Although Doris and Christine were together, they missed having their brothers with them, but most of all, they all missed Mamma. During the day, Doris knew she had to be grown-up. Aunt Jessie wasn't used to having children around and she needed Doris to help with Christine. At times Christine would cry just because she missed her mother. Doris had to try to comfort or distract her, the best she could.

The nights became the time when Doris could cry. She became very good at crying into her pillow without making any loud noises. She tried not to cry, but she missed her Mamma so much. So many things reminded her of Mamma, and the things that didn't, she'd catch herself thinking, *I'll have to tell Mamma about this after work*. During the days, she was strong and when she did helpful things, she'd assure herself that she was making her mother proud.

The winter mornings were so cold at Aunt Jessie and Uncle Bjarne's flat, that it was hard for Christine and Doris to get out of their bed and get ready for school. Jessie wasn't good about keeping them on schedule, like Mamma had been, and they were often late for school.

Spring was more comfortable, and on Easter, they got to take a trip with Pappa to visit their brothers at Tante Ulla's house.

During the "Summer Vacation," the boys still lived with Tante Ulla, but it was too far from Uncle Bjarne and Aunt Jessie for the girls to be able to play with them. At Aunt Jessie and Uncle Bjarne's flat, it was hot both inside and outside and there wasn't very much to keep Doris and Christine entertained. They were glad when school finally started again, but once they came home from school, their days had very little to make them happy.

Mamma's Sickness

The girls still missed their brothers and life as it was, when Mamma was there. Every day seemed to be the same. When the other children in their classes were excitedly looking forward to Christmas, Doris and Christine just felt sadder. Aunt Jessie never talked about going to church, or wrapping presents, or Christmas Cookies.

Magnus, Christine, Doris, Alert and Oscar

Chapter 4
A New Home For The Boys

Tante Ulla's mother-in-law came from Norway, to spend Christmas with her son and his family. Pappa never talked about the boys or Tante Ulla and Uncle Oscar with Doris and Christine, they just knew there was a long time between the times they saw them.

When Uncle Oscar's mother saw how much work Tante Ulla had caring for her own family and Oscar and Alert, she pressed Ulla to tell Magnus that he would have to make other arrangement for the boys.

Magnus was not healthy at this time, and the pressure to find a new home for the boys just a few weeks before Christmas, was far more than he was prepared to take on. He was working whenever his health permitted, and there was no way he could care for the boys, who were now two and a half and almost five years old.

Magnus visited orphan homes in Elizabeth, NJ, Brooklyn and Staten Island, NY. He talked to anyone who might have an answer for him. Pastor Bronsen, from the church Aagot brought the children to every Sunday morning, recommended an orphan home in Fort Lee,

NJ. "The Christian Orphan Home has been operating for many years," said Pastor Bronsen. "I have come to know several young people who had lived there and left to become successful in their lives, and ministries."

The word "ministries" wasn't especially appealing to Magnus, but he was desperate. "I know Father Nelson well," Pastor Bronsen told Magnus as he passed him a piece of paper on which he had written the name, address, and a phone number for the Orphan Home and the name of the man who was in charge there.

"Thank you very much," Magnus said, standing up to leave.

"I'm very sorry for you and your children, Magnus. Aagot was a very special young woman, and I know your loss is great."

"Thank you, again," said Magnus, fighting back his emotions at the painful reminder of his wife.

Waiting for a letter to get there and the response to be mailed back would take too long. Magnus called Father Nelson's office from a pay phone in the hallway of a neighbor's house and made an appointment to meet with him the next day.

The easiest way to get from Elizabeth to Fort Lee went through New York City, and took four hours. When he got off the last trolley, he saw that he still had to walk up a long, private road. Reminding himself of the importance of his mission propelled Magnus up that steep

road. There were woods on each side, and the trees were so close to the road that their branches met in the middle.

It was quiet; the air was clean and nothing was moving except an occasional squirrel jumping from branch to branch, but Magnus had difficulty finding beauty or enjoyment in anything. Although he had left enough time to look around the grounds, Magnus decided to save the little energy he had left for his trip home.

The big front door was easier to push open than its size indicated. The warmth felt good to Magnus as he stepped into the building and walked up three wide, light-colored wooden steps and into a large entry room. The center of the shiny wood floor was covered with a thin, dark maroon, woolen rug with wear spots at the doorways. In the front of the entry room, there were two very dramatic, wide, open staircases against the walls on each side of the entrance, curving toward the center of the room.

There were several armchairs with padded seats spaced out against the walls. To his right, there was an arched entrance to what appeared to be a living room. Straight ahead, a set of French doors offered a view of a covered porch beyond which, anyone knowing what to look for, could catch a glimpse of the NYC Skyline, through the bare treetops.

A slender, well-dressed gentleman of average height entered the entry room from an office behind a second set of French doors to Magnus's left. The man approached Magnus extending his hand.

"You must be Magnus. I am Father Nelson," is what the man said, but it was his strong Norwegian accent that reached deeply into Magnus's being, making him feel like he was in the right place.

The man continued, "I'm called Father Nelson. Father is not an official or liturgical title; it came from the children.

Most of them have no living father of their own. I am honored whenever I'm called Father Nelson."

"Nice to meet you, Father Nelson, I am Magnus Haukland. I am father to four children, but although they have a father who is still living, they no longer have a living mother, and unlike you, when they call me Pappa, frankly, right now, I feel a wave of inadequacy and sadness come over me. My health is not good, and without my wife to care for my children and me, I have been getting sicker and weaker in every way."

Father Nelson directed Magnus to a seat next to his desk, where Magnus lost no time continuing to tell his story. Father Nelson couldn't tell whether it was because Magnus was nervous, or embarrassed, or weak, but Magnus's head hung down and he seemed to focus on a spot on the rug as he continued.

"My sister-in-law has been caring for my two youngest children since their mother went into the hospital almost a year ago. They are Oscar, who is almost five, and Alert, who is almost two and a half. My wife, Aagot, passed away on January 21st of this year, then last week, Aagot's sister informed me that she would like me to find someplace else for the boys to live, as soon as possible."

Magnus then addressed concerns about his older children. "My wife's brother and his wife have been looking after my daughters. Doris is eight and a half years old and Christine is six and will be seven in March. The older one is very mature for her age. She cares for herself completely, and when she's not in school, she does most of the care for her sister, as well. When all the children were still at home and my wife was not well, Doris was caring for the whole family, with her mother's direction. Even though there is not a lot of physical care needed for the girls, the couple caring for them never had children of their own, and they are uncomfortable having this responsibility. I am certain this arrangement will probably not last much longer, either."

Raising his head and making eye contact with Father Nelson assured Magnus that he had Father Nelson's complete attention. Father Nelson nodded in understanding, and in a very caring, gentle manner, said, "Magnus, you are carrying a load that is much too heavy for one man! What can I do to help you?"

Relieved to have voiced even just some of the painful matters that he had been holding inside him for these past months, and appreciative of Father Nelson's affirmation of the seriousness of his concerns, Magnus's head raised and his shoulders relaxed as he sat back into the chair. He continued in a more calm voice, maintaining eye contact with Father Nelson.

"I have looked at many orphan homes, and spoken to agencies about foster care. When Pastor Bronsen told me about your home, I began talking to as many people as I could about it. I have heard so many good reports and nothing bad. I have heard that the children who live here are happy and well adjusted while they are here, and even after they leave."

"That's good to hear, Magnus. As I told you, my wife and I have no children of our own. In 1900, at the same time we had become concerned about several young children we saw wandering on their own in Journal Square, Jersey City, several men from our church shared the same concern. We got together and established a place for them to call home, where we could teach them of the Love of God. When a woman with five children, asked to have all of her children placed with us, we began to look for a larger home, outside Jersey City. A doctor had built this large, beautiful building as a gift for his bride, but she refused to move here, saying it was too far from anywhere. It is perfect for us."

Magnus knew that Aagot would love to have her children living where they would learn more about God.

Resolved in his hope that this was the best solution available, Magnus thought *I have been giving Aagot's sister and brother money to help pay for food and a little extra for other expenses. Between that and my own rent and expenses, I have very little left at the end of the month.* "What does it cost for the children to live here?" he asked.

The answer Father Nelson had to give Magnus conflicted strongly with his personal desire to be helpful. When Father Nelson hesitated, Magnus knew it was because what he was about to say, was going to be very difficult for both of them. In a timid effort to ease the pressure, Magnus asked, "What would it cost for just the boys?"

Father Nelson was coming to realize more and more that Magnus's struggles went beyond the emotional pain related to loss of his wife, and the need for a suitable, long-term arrangement for his children's care. Magnus looked like a man who was not healthy. It was obvious that it took a great deal of effort for him to keep his job and to meet his financial responsibilities. Father Nelson struggled to balance what he knew it cost per child to meet the expenses, with what he was sensing Magnus would be able to afford, but now his position required that he give an answer. Father Nelson wrote the figures on a slip of paper and handed it to Magnus.

Magnus didn't respond immediately. He was mentally calculating what he was able to afford. *He would still have to give Bjarne and Jessie money to help out with the girls, and meet his own expenses, but he hated to pass up this opportunity. Perhaps if the worry of his sons's well being was lifted from his mind, he would be better able to take on more work.*

Father Nelson broke the silence of this already uncomfortable moment, saying, "There is still another concern that I will have to address. The nurse in charge of the group of children we call Tots, has asked that I not take in any children who are still in diapers. Is your younger son still in diapers?"

Magnus was glad that Father Nelson realized the possibility that Alert was still wearing diapers, yet he was still considering his proposal.

"Yes, Father Nelson, Alert still wears diapers. As you said, he is still young, and his Aunt hasn't attempted to work with him on this, as she has had more than enough to handle between her own family, and my two youngsters."

"I understand," said Father Nelson. "I will talk with Miss Flotten as soon as I can, and see if she will work with us on this matter."

With the hope of solving his greatest immediate need, a home for the boys, and the potential to eventually have all four children here, together, Magnus noticed a relaxation of the tightness he had been feeling in his chest, and his breathing now required less effort. Although he didn't verbalize his thoughts, Magnus believed he could agree to meet this financial commitment. *If the woman will just agree to take a "Tot" in diapers, this could be the answer I have been searching for.*

"Well, let's see," said Father Nelson, taking out a book that had lists of children divided according to their ages, and the room they were in. "I think we could fit one more bed and one more crib into this room. Would you be able to wait here while I go over to the other building and speak with Miss Flotten? If you'd like to see the other building, you are welcome to join me."

Father Nelson's invitation alone was enough assurance to Magnus that the Superintendent didn't have anything to hide. Although he was feeling quite a bit better than when he arrived, Magnus chose to wait in Father Nelson's office for his return. As he left the room, Father Nelson said, "I'll see if there's anyone in the kitchen who would be able to bring you a cup of coffee."

Magnus sat staring out the window, torn between trying to process what was ahead of him and using these few minutes to relax. He was startled when an older woman, entered the room and asked, with a strong Norwegian accent, "Mr. Haukland, do you want sugar or cream with your coffee?"

"Nay Takk," Magnus answered, in Norwegian.

The woman smiled broadly, setting the sugar and cream back on the tray. Slipping gladly into speaking Norwegian, she introduced herself as Olga and offered Magnus an assortment of open-faced sandwiches that appeared to have been prepared for him.

Olga explained that she had come from Norway eight years ago, and has been working at The Home, as a cook, since then. She spoke of the acceptance and generosity of the local community toward The Home, the happiness of the children, their summers at camp, and about the love of Jesus that she felt since she had made this her new home.

"I see you two have met," Father Nelson said, smiling. The time had gone by so quickly; it was hard to believe he had ever left the building. Olga filled Magnus's cup then poured a cup of coffee for Father Nelson, before she excused herself saying, in English, that she had to get back to preparing dinner.

"Well," said Father Nelson, "Miss Flotten has agreed to take JUST ONE child in diapers, especially with the hope that your older daughter may be coming soon to help out with her brother."

Magnus could hardly contain the relief he felt with those words. He thanked Father Nelson, and asked if it would be all right if he brought the money with him every other week when he came to visit the boys.

Father Nelson was agreeable to this, and said, "Magnus, I will have the maintenance man set up a bed and a crib in the corner of the room, so the boys will be able to see each other all the time. You can bring them here any time tomorrow."

Strengthened by the sandwiches, encouraged by Olga's conversation, relieved that Aagot's sister would no longer be burdened by his sons, and as close to hopeful as Magnus remembered being for months, he stood up several inches taller than when he arrived and said, "Tusen Takk (A Thousand Thanks), from the bottom of my heart," to Father Nelson.

Father and Mother Nelsen

All arrangements were quickly made. Although Tante Ulla also lived in Elizabeth, Magnus had to take several trolleys to get to their house. Tante Ulla had packed a few things for the boys to take with them, but she couldn't bear to watch them leave. It had been a year since they first came to live with her, and by now both of them thought of her as their mother. Her husband Oscar had a car, so he drove Magnus and the boys to The Home.

The boys were too young to understand what was happening. Although the words wanted to choke him rather than come out of his mouth, Magnus spoke gently to his son: "Oscar, you and Alert are going to be in a big new house, now, with lots of other children."

"Why?" Oscar asked.

"This will be a place where your sisters Doris and Christine can someday come to live, too."

"But why?" He asked again.

Magnus didn't know any answers to give Oscar, and Alert was too young to even ask questions, so as gently as they could, the two men brought the two little boys upstairs in the big brick building, and they were all introduced to Tootsie, a young girl who helped with the Tots. They placed their things on the rocking chair between what would now be their bed and crib.

Tootsie was pleasant and tried to get Oscar and Alert to come to her, but neither of them would. Tootsie suggested they all get some ice cream in the dining room downstairs, and while they were eating she talked with the boys, primarily addressing Oscar. She told him about the other children who lived at The Home, and games they would play. She listened as Oscar told her that he liked to play hockey and ride a tricycle.

When they finished their ice cream, Tootsie invited Oscar and Alert to come and see the little playroom just down the hall. After a few minutes, they became interested in the toys, and Magnus and Uncle Oscar slipped out.

Magnus's heart nearly broke. He didn't cry, but the lump in his throat didn't allow him to talk, either. The ride back was long and silent, and Magnus was glad when Oscar let him out right at his flat.

Chapter 5
Doris's Promise

*O*nce he was home, Magnus cried with deep sobs that didn't want to stop. He hated leaving the boys without saying goodbye, but he knew that was the only way he could have left. They were just too young to understand.

Mornings were cold in the empty flat. Magnus forced himself out of bed and added enough coal to the fading fire in the big iron stove in the kitchen, to heat a pot of water to use for bathing, shaving and a cup of coffee. He kept just enough food in the icebox to maintain his strength. It was painfully lonely to be in the flat that used to be filled with life and kept warm and welcoming by his wife. Other than sleeping, bathing, eating and packing his lunch, there was no reason for Magnus to maintain a home for just himself. As soon as he was dressed, he went to the neighbor's house and called Father Nelson, to ask how his sons were.

Father Nelson arranged to call Magnus back in ten minutes, so he would be able to speak with Miss Flotten, who was the nurse for the Tots.

When he called back, he said, "Miss Flotten said Alert cried for about an hour before he fell asleep, and in the morning, they found that Oscar had climbed into the crib, and they were sleeping quietly, together."

Father Nelson assured Magnus that his boys would adjust, just as others had. That was little comfort to Magnus, but he saw no other option. The best he could hope for was to move ahead with thoughts of having the girls move to The Home where all four children could be together for the first time in over a year.

Working long days had left little time for him to see any of his children, even though the girls were just down the street from his flat. Christmas, was in the air, but not in his heart, and barely on his mind. Aagot always made sure the children had special clothes to wear to church on Christmas, and though they had little money for toys, there would always be a little package for each of his children to open. This year, Magnus was so occupied with changes for his children and trying to be a dependable employee, that Christmas seemed to come and go without any mention of celebration. As he was on his way home from work in the evenings, he would look to see if the light in the room where his little girls slept was still on. If it was, Magnus would stop to say good night to them. That always made his day a little brighter, but once they were asleep, Bjarne would bring up subjects related to returning to life without Magnus's children in his home.

Bjarne worked on a tugboat, and he would often be gone for several days in a row. When he arrived home, he wanted the privacy and simplicity of the life that he had been used to. Recently, Bjarne added that he was concerned about his wife being too tired after taking care of the girls.

Jessie was a simple woman. Bjarne told Magnus that he was quite certain that having the girls there was too difficult for his wife to do much longer. She and Bjarne were happy together, but taking care of herself and Bjarne seemed to be all Jessie could comfortably handle. Aunt Jessie had kept Christine, for a few hours after school when Aagot was still working, but even then, she paid little attention to Christine, and was unable to discipline her. Christine sometimes entertained herself, by climbing up the exposed pipes in Aunt Jessie's flat.

When he returned to his own flat, Magnus wrapped himself in blankets, and lay in his cold, un-made bed. As tired as he was, he knew that he had to come up with a plan.

Tante Ulla's sister-in-law lived in a large home, in Brooklyn, with her husband and their son, Jon. Many times since Aagot had passed away, she told Magnus that she had an extra room in her house, and she invited him to come and live with them. She was a very kind and caring woman, but he hadn't considered moving into her home, seriously, until now. He didn't want to impose on her or her family, and at least he was near the girls in Elizabeth. But now it was time to consider this.

Magnus thought to himself, *I have been surviving, but at the expense of others. It's time to get my whole family settled in a more permanent place. If Jessie is having as much difficulty as Bjarne feels she is, it is not good for the girls to be in her care.* Before falling into a deep sleep, Magnus resolved that in the morning, he would speak to Tante Ulla's Sister-In-Law, Mrs. Boardsen, about the empty room in her house. Then on Saturday, he would go visit the boys and speak to Father Nelson about moving the girls up to The Home, as soon as possible.

On Saturday morning, his body ached from the long week of working on the docks, and even though it was difficult, he forced himself out of bed. Once he was dressed, he used the phone in his neighbor's hall to call

Mrs. Boardsen. Once that was done, he prepared for his trip to The Home. Since it was a weekend, he would probably find a seat on the ferries, trains and trolleys he would use on his four-hour trip to The Home. Just the trip took a lot out of him, and every moment was filled trying to work out details of the plans and thoughts of what he could do to make the lives of his children the best they could be.

When he arrived at The Home and saw his little sons looking so lost among all the other children, it tore at his already broken heart. He scooped them up in his arms and sat, holding back tears, as he gently hummed a familiar song to them. Alert fell asleep in his arms, and Oscar slid onto the floor and moved on to playing with a toy car. Magnus eased Alert into the crib, kissed Oscar on his head as he continued to play, and ended his visit. He knew then, that it was right for the children to be together at this Home.

Speaking with Father Nelson was easier than he anticipated. With a hot cup of coffee in their hands, the men spoke openly about the situation. Father Nelson once again assured Magnus that the boys would soon be acclimated to their new setting, but when he calculated the cost of having the girls come to the Home, too, it was more than Magnus would be able to pay, even if his health improved, and he gave up his flat. After speaking for close to an hour, Father Nelson proposed that if the eldest daughter who was eight and a half years old would be able to regularly assist in the care of the youngest boy, he would reduce the total cost.

The new figure, although still high, would leave Magnus with enough money to buy food for himself, pay for transportation and pay a very small amount for the room he would move into. With a strong handshake, agreement was reached, and the girls would be coming as soon as they were ready.

This morning, when he spoke with Mrs. Boardsen, she sounded very happy that Magnus had decided to come and live with them in Brooklyn. Now he was feeling a lot more comfortable with this plan, too. It would not only cost a lot less than the flat he was living in, but traveling to visit the children and to get to his job would both be a lot easier from Mrs. Boardsen's house.

Magnus planned to go right to Bjarne's home and speak to Doris. Even at her young age, Doris would understand what had to be done and she would be able to manage Christine, who was more self-centered and more likely to have a tantrum when she was told about the change.

It was now the end of December, and although there were only patches of dirty snow here and there along the cobblestone streets of Elizabeth, it felt cold enough to snow more at any moment. Still, Magnus needed to talk with Doris alone.

With Christine busily playing with her doll in the living room, Magnus motioned to Doris to come to him. "Doris," he said, in his Norwegian accent, "I would like to talk to you, alone. Would you come and take a walk with me?"

He helped her put the only coat she had on. There was a mitten that her mother had knit, in each pocket. A long, matching string went up one sleeve, across the back and down the other sleeve. He tenderly took them out of the pockets and helped her slip one hand into each mitten. He then wrapped the somewhat unusual scarf that she had knit by herself, with different colored scraps of wool, over her head and around her neck.

Magnus used hand motions to tell Aunt Jessie what they were up to, and then Magnus and Doris slipped out the door and down the dark, wooden staircase.

Doris seemed to enjoy "sneaking" out, and she and her father were snickering under their breath, as they tried to minimize the squeaking of the old steps. The playful spirit of his precious daughter was somehow comforting to Magnus, and even though this was yet another difficult situation to deal with, Doris's unwavering love and trust in him made this time together one in which Magnus felt more like a responsible adult and loving father than he had, in a very long time.

They walked for several blocks, then mutually decided to rest on a park bench. Magnus began speaking slowly and gently.

"Doris, do you remember what Mamma said to you when you saw her in the hospital?"

"Yes," she answered. "She told me to keep the family together."

It became obvious that although she knew the words, she had no concept of what the words might mean, and what her roll would be in keeping that promise. Magnus affirmed her recollection and praised her for remembering.

He continued. "The boys have moved from Tante Ulla's house to a special Home with lots of other children. I went to see the boys today. They look very sad and lonely at The Home. I was wondering if you and Christine would go and live there with them. Then even though I wouldn't live there with you, you could all be together, and I could come and visit you all every other Sunday. I will be moving too, Doris. I am going to move to Brooklyn, to live with Tante Ulla's sister-in-law, Mrs. Boardsen. I will no longer live in the house we lived in when Mamma was with us."

Doris loved the house they lived in before Mamma died. It was just down the street from Aunt Jessie's house, so she passed it often. She would miss living in Elizabeth. As she sat quietly beside him, with steam coming off her breath, Magnus could almost sense that Doris, who was always eager to do what was helpful, was beginning to make a connection between her mother's words and moving to The Home with the other children.

"Pappa, would we all sleep in the same room?"

"No, Doris, the boys will live in a different building, but it will be close and during the day, when they are not in school, the children get together to play."

"Oh, but Christine and I will be together?"

"Yes, you will probably even be in the same bed, just like you have always been. You and Christine will sleep in a big beautiful house where there are 25 other girls. Some of them are around your age and the oldest girls there are 13 years old."

"And we can play with Oscar and Alert during the day?"

"Yes," he repeated, "except when you are at school. You and Christine will go to school from there, just like you do here, only the school is a little further from The Home than it is from the house in Elizabeth."

With just a moment's pause, Doris announced, "Okay Pappa, Christine and I will go there to live near the boys."

Magnus's eyes filled with tears, but the courageous answer from his little daughter with the big understanding forced him to hold back the tears, and a soft smile spread on his face as he said, "Doris, I am very proud of you, and I know that Mamma is very happy with all you do to help Aunt Jessie, Christine and me. I think you will be happy at The Home once you get used to it, and I know the boys will be happier if you are there. Father Nelson is the man who is in charge there, and he told me that it doesn't take too long until the children get used to living there, and then they are very happy."

Rooted

On the way back to Aunt Jessie's, Doris asked more questions, and Pappa told her more about the buildings and the other children he had seen there. He asked her if she could get Christine's and her own things packed by tomorrow morning. By now, she was getting so excited at the thought; she assured him that she and Christine would be ready first thing in the morning.

That night, when she told Christine her bedtime story, it was about four children who lived in a very big house on the top of a hill. The house had a playroom and outside it had its very own playground. For a while Christine's eyes widened and she too became excited, but gradually, sleep over-came the excitement, and Doris was able to stop telling a story, and start thinking to herself, about what it would be like to live in the new place. *It will be sad to leave Aunt Jessie and Uncle Bjarne, and my teacher and classmates, but there are no other children to play with near Aunt Jessie's and Christine doesn't always play nicely. Maybe I'll meet a new friend there.*

There were no tears that night. Her pillow would be dry. There was hope and a comforting feeling of obeying her mother that allowed Doris to pull up the covers and drift into a good night sleep, not even aware of when Pappa left.

When the girls went to bed, Magnus sat at the dining room table, explaining his plans to Jessie and Bjarne. Although Jessie tried to deny the strain that caring for the girls had been on her, she and Bjarne couldn't help but agree that it would be best if all of the children were together.

Chapter 6
Moving – Almost Together

*I*t was barely light outside when Aunt Jessie handed Doris two pillowcases to fill with their things. They each had a Sunday dress and Sunday shoes, play clothes, a few dresses to wear to school, and a pair of warm pajamas. Each had a doll that was three inches tall.

"Doris, what are the pillow cases for?" Christine asked.

"Christine, do you remember the story I told you before we went to sleep last night, about four children who were going to all live in a big building together?" Doris asked.

"Yes. It sounded like it would be fun," Christine said.

"Well, that story was a little like what is going to happen today. Oscar and Alert have already moved into a big building on top of a hill, and you and I are going to move into a different building – one for girls- that is also at the top of the hill.

"Does Pappa know?" Christine asked.

"Yes," Doris answered. "He will be taking us there, today."

"What about Aunt Jessie and Uncle Bjarne?" Christine asked.

"They will go back to living together the way they used to," Doris explained.

"Are you sure Pappa knows about this?" Christine asked.

Doris chuckled. "Yes, I'm sure. He'll probably be here soon, to take us to our new home where we will live near Oscar and Alert."

Even though they weren't going to church this morning, it was Sunday, so they decided to wear their Sunday outfits. Since Pappa told Doris there would be a lot of walking, and their Sunday shoes hurt a lot when they walked in them, they each put on a pair of socks and the shoes they wore everyday.

When Magnus arrived around eight o'clock, both girls were packed, had finished their breakfast and were ready to leave. He sat at the dining room table and enjoyed a cup of hot coffee and a slice of bread with butter.

Before they left, Magnus and the girls said a great big thank you to Aunt Jessie and Uncle Bjarne. As they walked down the dark, squeaky steps, all three of them giggled under their breath as they forced each step to make as much noise as it would.

First they got on a trolley car, then a ferry, next a train, then another ferryboat, two more trains and another trolley. The trip took four hours, and although they were getting tired and hungry, the excitement was too great to think about being tired or hungry.

Finally, instead of *almost,* which Pappa was answering each time the girls asked if they were there yet, now he said, "Ja. This is where we get off the trolley and we will walk the rest of the way."

Magnus stepped down out of the trolley, and holding all of the girls's possessions in one hand, he reached back for the hands of each of his daughters, one at a time. Right behind their Pappa was a huge stone pillar with a sign that Doris easily read: "The Christian Orphan Home for Children." On the other side of a country road, was a second stone pillar with a sign that said 1512 Palisade Avenue.

With an encouraging, "Let's go, girls, we're almost there," Magnus pointed up the road. There was still snow on the sides of the road and in the woods, but it was white instead of black like the snow in Elizabeth. The road started off kind of level, and they couldn't see any buildings from where they were.

Looking deep into the woods, Christine asked, "Where are the other houses and the stores?"

"There are no stores close to here, but soon you'll see the buildings," Pappa answered.

Stone (Girls) Building

When they got to the bottom of a steep hill, they looked up and saw a big, stone building. Doris remembered how Pappa had described the building as looking like a house in a fairy tale. There were lots of big, frosty windows and an inviting entry. On one side of the building, there was a large, covered porch. There was smoke coming out of the chimney and disappearing into the sky above the house. This one building was larger than 6 whole flats, in Elizabeth. It was beautiful.

It was a good thing this was the end of their trip, because it was definitely the hardest part. Their little legs (and Pappa's big ones) ached as they went up the steep part of the road.

Pappa pushed open the front door, and they all laughed and groaned as they forced their tired legs to climb up three wide, light-colored wooden steps that brought them into a large, open entry room. After their long trip, they appreciated the warmth of the building, and they were delighted by the familiarity of the song being played on a piano in the next room. There were many wooden doors with glass panes in them, leading to other rooms, and one set of doors led to a porch in the back of the building. There were several cushioned chairs in the room and a big clock, ticking loudly as its pendulum swung back and forth. The floor was covered in the middle by a maroon rug with tassels on two sides.

Almost right away, a man came through one of the glass doors, and gave Pappa a hearty handshake. "It's good to see you again, so soon, Magnus," he said. Then he bent forward so his face was at their level, and introduced himself to Christine and Doris. He shook each of their hands, saying, "Welcome. We're so glad you are coming to live with us here."

The girls couldn't wait to see their brothers, and everything else inside and out, but first, they would learn where they would sleep, starting tonight.

The music stopped and the woman who had been playing the piano walked over to meet them. Father Nelson introduced her to the girls:

"Miss Bersager, this is Doris Haukland, and this is Christine Haukland. Girls, this is Miss Bersager, she is the nurse who takes care of the all the girls. Miss Bersager, would you please show the girls their room?"

Miss Bersager knew right away where to go and which bed had been made for them. Turning around to follow her, they saw the most beautiful staircase they had ever seen. It was actually two staircases, both with very wide, shiny, light colored wooden steps, and a matching wooden railing attached to white spindles. The stairs were against the walls on opposite sides of the entry room, one on each side of the entrance to the room, and the steps curved toward each other, as they rose, though they didn't meet. They both ended at a landing. The girls couldn't see that from down stairs, but once they reached the landing, there was a big window made up of smaller panes of glass. Christine couldn't keep herself from running ahead and kneeling on the padded bench beneath the window that went from one side of the landing to the other.

Looking out of the huge, window, she said, "Look, Doris, there's the road we just climbed up!" Miss Bersager, smiled, as if she understood Christine's excitement, then they all turned and continued up the rest of the steps that were opposite the bench, between the two stair cases that came up from the entry room. In the excitement, both of the girls totally forgot how tired their legs had felt just a short time ago.

There were three large, separate rooms on this floor. Doris and Christine would be in the largest room, which had ten beds. Christine and Doris had always slept in the same bed, so Miss Bersager had only made one new bed for both of them. They would have the bed at the end of the room, in front of the radiator.

Miss Bersager then showed them the room for the next oldest girls. There were eight neatly made beds there, for girls between nine and eleven years old, and in the "big girls" room, there were six neatly made beds, some with stuffed animals on them. The big girls were twelve and thirteen.

Before they went down stairs, Miss Bersager showed them the bathroom, and asked if they wanted to use it. The sisters looked at each other and giggled. It had been a long time since they left Aunt Jessie's house, and they were glad for Miss Bersager's thoughtfulness. There was one bathroom with one toilet for twenty-five girls, but right now there were only two of them. It was the first time they had used a bathroom that had a sink, a toilet and a tub.

When they came back down the steps, they held tightly to the rail. The depth of each step was different from the next, as the staircase curved around, and they were only used to steps that were all the same. Father Nelson and Pappa were sitting in the cushioned chairs, drinking coffee. The calm appearance of both men, and Pappa's comfort with Father Nelson re-assured the girls that this was just the right place to be.

Father Nelson said, "I was just about to go over to the dining room. Perhaps you would join me for lunch. The children are just finishing their meal, and maybe I'll be able to answer any questions you young ladies or your father have, and tell you a little more about our Home while we're eating."

Pappa seemed almost embarrassed to be hungry, and even though the girls were both hungry, too, all they wanted to know at the moment was:

"Where are our brothers and when can we see them?"

Father Nelson smiled, warmly, and said, "Well, the dining room is in the building that the Tots are in, so let's head over that way." With that, the girls put on their coats, and the foursome left the big, stone building. There was a little road leading up to another large building. This one was a brick building, and they would only have to walkup five cement steps to get in.

Brick (Boys') Building

As they were getting closer to the brick building, the door suddenly flew open and what seemed like a huge wave of children of all sizes poured out of the door and down the steps. Some went off in a different direction, but most of them headed straight toward Father Nelson, Pappa, Doris and Christine. It was almost frightening. They weren't even watching where they were going. They were loud - lots of laughing and talking and calling to one another. No one really stared at the newcomers, but many of them waved and called, "Hello Father Nelson," as they passed.

Entering the brick building felt comfortable to the girls right away. There was the delicious smell of food, the noise of clanging dishes - glasses and silverware, and children laughing and talking loudly to each other. Down a short hall and to the right was the dining room. The room was mostly empty. There were a few teenagers gathering the last of the dishes and clearing off the tables, and in the far corner of the room, there was one last diner, and his assistant.

The last diner was Alert! He was sitting in a high chair with a girl who was about twelve or thirteen years old, in front of him. The girl was wearing a dirty towel fastened around her neck and hanging down to her knees, and everywhere that wasn't covered by the towel was also splattered with food. It was in her hair, on her arms, all over the floor and the chair.

Pappa had told Doris that Alert was unhappy, but that's not what they witnessed. Alert was laughing and spitting and seemed to be thoroughly enjoying the mess he was making.

The Hauklands were embarrassed. Instinctively, Doris ran toward Alert and the girl, and she apologized to the girl. Alert grinned slyly at Doris, then he reached out his hands, asking to be held by her. It was hard to resist this adorable boy with the gravy in his long blond curls, but before she would pick him up, he had to be cleaned-up.

Doris went right to work. The young girl was happy to bring her dampened rags, then dry ones, and she took off the towel that Alert had draped across his chest and lap, which was also almost covered with food.

Pappa apologized to Father Nelson; "I hope this isn't a regular behavior for Alert."

Father Nelson, didn't look directly at Pappa, nor answer him right away, but then he said, "Some of the Tots who can't talk yet, find different ways to express themselves. At first, Alert didn't want to eat anything, so the girls that fed him tried to make eating fun. He came to enjoy the game. It seems that he gets more of the food on the children feeding him and his surroundings than into his body, but we are happy that he is at least eating some of the food." It looked like Doris would definitely be earning the money that was taken off the bill for her room and board.

"Dottie," said Father Nelson to the young lady who had been feeding Alert, "This is Mr. Haukland, Oscar and Alert's father, and these are his daughters, Doris and Christine. They will be moving into The Home today!"

Dottie smiled and said, "It's nice to meet you, Mr. Haukland." Then bubbling with excitement, she turned to Christine and Doris and said, "Welcome. You are going to love it here, and your brothers are going to be so happy you're here!"

"Dottie, would you please go upstairs and bring Oscar back to the dining room?" Father Nelson asked. Dottie hurried out of the room and up the stairs to get Oscar.

When she returned with Oscar, he was rubbing his eyes, as he had just fallen asleep for a nap. Once he recognized his sisters, he pulled his hand from Dottie. He ran and wrapped his arms around Christine, and then he ran and hugged Doris who was already holding Alert. Then he hugged Pappa before he spun around in a circle, jumping up and down clapping his hands.

That sealed any doubt Magnus had about the decision to put all of his children in this Home. Within the first five minutes of being together, Alert calmed down, and Oscar came to life.

Father Nelson, the girls and their Pappa sat at a table that had been cleared and set for them. Father Nelson closed his eyes, and folded his hands, so the girls and Pappa did the same. Father Nelson said, "Father, bless the food we are about to eat, to our bodies, and bless us to your service. Amen"

When they opened their eyes, a teenage boy brought out bowls of gravy, mashed potatoes, ground meat, green beans and carrots. They each helped themselves, and Pappa helped Christine, when she looked like she was struggling. The boys played on the floor around them. Pappa and Father Nelson were pleased as they watched Alert occasionally take a spoon of meat or vegetables from Christine and Doris.

As they ate, Father Nelson continued to calmly tell the girls what to expect on a regular day and that tomorrow he would drive them both to school. Looking up from his plate, Father Nelson realized that the girls were torn between hearing what he was saying, and celebrating the beginning of their renewed bonding as sisters and brothers. It was plain to him that it was only because the children were well mannered, that they continued to listen to him at all.

"Go ahead and enjoy your dinner, children," said Father Nelson, "You'll have lots of time to learn everything there is to know about your new Home."

Once he stopped talking, he quietly watched the children.

Christine huddled next to Oscar on the floor, and quietly, she told him; "Doris and I are moving into the other big building over there, today!"

Os didn't seem to fully understand what Christine was saying, but he could see in her eyes that it was something very, very good.

Father Nelson felt privileged to be able to observe this broken family not only renewing their relationships, but also knitting itself into a new entity. Especially noticeable was the blossoming of the eight and a half year old, young lady. Her mother had obviously been a wonderful role model, and had prepared her young daughter for great things. Doris did not realize that she was more than a big sister to the others, but without a word said about it, all of them seemed to be accepting Doris as the one to hold this new unit together.

When they left the dining room, it was cloudy and a light snow was falling. Pappa would have to begin his long trip home, so he decided to leave right away. The girls were eager to see where the boy's beds were, so Pappa kissed each one goodbye, and promised to come and see them *not next Sunday, but the Sunday after that.* He would come after they had their dinner, in the middle of the day.

All four children stood at the doorway calling, "Goodbye," and waving as Pappa walked down the little road, toward the big house, with Father Nelson.

Standing face to face in front of the stone building, Father Nelson again shook Pappa's hand. Then he put his other hand on Pappa's shoulder. The children watched as their Pappa and Father Nelson seemed to be looking down at the ground. Soon they looked at each other again and then Pappa turned and headed down the steep hill in front of the big house.

Once he was out of sight, the children shrieked with excitement. Becoming bolder and more comfortable in the new setting. They finished peeking into every open door on the first floor, and then headed up a flight of stairs to find Oscar and Alert's beds.

Walking cautiously down the steep hill with the light coating of snow, Magnus found the silence oppressive, much more bothersome than the loudest noises of all the children. The beauty of the canopy of branches above him, outlined with the newly falling snow, was totally wasted on Magnus. Everything inside him wanted to SCREAM.

He didn't see anyone, and he was quite sure no one would hear him if he did allow himself to let it all out, but he restrained himself nonetheless. From the depths of his being, in his restrained voice, he cried: "Aagot! How can I go on without you?" Tears flowed freely and he sobbed with all of the little strength he had. It was hard for him to remain on his feet, but the only fallen tree he could sit on was already wet with snow. He stood by the side of the road, struggling to pull himself together. He reminded himself that he needed to catch the trolley, but he was unable to move. "Aagot," he started again, "I believe with all my heart that this is the best thing I could do for the children right now. You know that I am not well. Soon they will be settled here. You see how happy they are to be together, and the other children who are living here already, seem very well adjusted and happy.

"Aagot, when I left Father Nelson, he prayed - he talked to God, just like you used to do. He asked God to bless our children and their lives here, and to bless me as I travel home and struggle to know that I have made the right decision. Aagot, not only will our children be together and have food and be warm, they will also learn more of what you were teaching them about God. Father Nelson told us that every day there will be devotions, singing and Bible stories, and on Sunday, all of the children will have Sunday School in their little Chapel. I would give anything if you were still with us and we could be in our little flat in Elizabeth, but I believe this will be a good home for our children."

Magnus paused trying to regain his strength, then he added a prayer to the God he heard Aagot teach their children about.

"God, I wish I learned more about you from Aagot, but right now, I want to thank you for Father Nelson and this Home. Please keep my children both safe and happy."

With that, he straightened his collar, brushed some of the snow off his shoulders, stood up as straight as he could, and finished the walk down the road where he caught the trolley, just before it pulled away.

55

Chapter 7
Settling In

The Haukland children were so focused on each other that they barely noticed the others around them. The boys were happy to show their sisters the things they had been playing with, and the girls were happy to see where their brothers were living. Except for one visit, when Pappa brought the girls to Tante Ulla's house on Easter, all four children had not been together for over a year.

The other children around them were so busy playing by themselves or with each other that they barely noticed the *new girls*. Doris wondered if it would be all right to bring the boys over to their building, but she didn't see any adults to ask for permission. Doris recognized Alert's snow suit and Oscar's coat which were hanging on low hooks near the door, so she got them both dressed, and she and Christine walked with them over to the big stone building.

The boys knew this building, because downstairs, was a large playroom. Oscar showed his sisters around the playroom. It was kind of crowded, so they decided to bring the boys up stairs to see their bed and the big bathroom.

For the first time they looked out the window on the back of the building. Through the falling snow and the snow-covered branches, they could see the big buildings of New York City. In the morning, they would look again, but for now, they chose to continue exploring inside.

All four children were engrossed in a game of hide and seek when suddenly a loud bell rang. Doris and Christine were startled. Oscar calmly said, "We need to go back to eat." The three older children put their winter coats on and Alert was buttoned into his snowsuit. Holding hands, and sticking their tongues out to catch the falling snowflakes, they headed back to the brick house for supper.

The Haukland children were walking in the same direction as the other boys and girls and Doris noted to herself, that they blended quite well with the other children. The littlest ones seemed to be around Alert's age, the biggest ones looked like the girl who helped Alert in the dining room, and there were lots in-between. Along with the other children were some older boys who were wearing very big mittens, and carrying very big pots. The pots were covered with lids and they had a handle on each side. It took two boys to carry each of the pots - one on each side. The boys kept calling out, "Coming through with Hot Pots!"

Tables were all set with plates, glasses and spoons, and the room was warm and it smelled good. The children seemed to know where to go - even Oscar and Alert. Dottie was waiting, with a clean towel, ready to do battle with Alert again.

When Doris said, "I'll feed him," Dottie was more than happy to give her the towel and the food that had been specially prepared for him. She had already planned a spot for Doris and Christine, at the table with the boys.

Rooted

Miss Bersager came into the room and said, "Good evening. After supper, there will be singing in the living room of the big house." Then she looked down and closed her eyes and said, "Father please bless the food that we are about to receive, we thank you and ask you to bless those who have prepared it and those who eat it. Amen." When she had finished, the room remained quiet.

Doris was giving all her attention to Alert, and Christine was actually helping Oscar with his food. They didn't really notice what was going on in the rest of the room. When Christine said, "Oscar, do you want more milk?" he looked surprised and almost horrified. He didn't answer her. She finally said, "What's the matter, Oscar, why won't you talk to me?" He still didn't say a word, but he pointed around the room.

Christine didn't have any idea what was happening. None of the children were speaking, but all or almost all of the children's fingers were wiggling up and down, back and forth, almost like they were playing the piano in the air. She nudged Doris and whispered, "What are they doing?" Doris was also puzzled by what was going on in the room, but for the rest of the meal, neither Doris nor Christine did any more talking.

Dotty walked by, and was amazed that Alert was eating! He opened his mouth for each spoonful of food and ate it without spitting any out. Dottie's mouth dropped open and she went and brought out another girl, who was in the kitchen, to show her. Doris and Alert looked very proud of their performance, but still no one said a word.

After dinner, Miss Bersager returned to the room, and told everyone they were dismissed. All of a sudden, chairs were scraping on the floor and everyone started to leave the room. They were all talking at once and the noise was as loud as thunder!

As Dottie was walking past to bring the dishes into the kitchen, Doris mustered up the courage to ask her; "Why wasn't anyone talking during the meal?"

Dottie answered in a voice loud enough to be heard over all the other children's voices, "It would be too noisy if everyone was allowed to call across the room to each other, so the children made-up their own sign language. They talk with their fingers. If one of the girls wants someone to pass something, she uses the sign language to ask for it. If she wants to tell someone something about school or anything else, she just spells it out with her fingers. Each letter of the alphabet has a finger position." Doris smiled and decided she was ready for the challenge of learning another language. She didn't realize she was already fluent in English and Norwegian.

The Hauklands were among the last to leave the dining room, but they still had enough time to walk back to the big building before the singing started. Having things to do was fun, and going from building to building, made the activities even more exciting, even if they did get cold and wet.

A pretty, young lady dressed in a red dress and wearing shoes that had high heels, was playing the piano in the parlor. Children were sitting all over the floor. The Hauklands found a spot that would fit four, and settled there. Doris was reminded of when Mamma used to play for them, at the neighbors house. They even knew some of the songs and sang along.

When the singing was over Miss Flotten, the nurse for the Tots, and her helper, Tootsie, were there to help bring the Tots back to the brick building and get them ready for bed. Christine and Doris kissed their brothers good night. Alert resisted when Tootsie took him from his sister's arms. Doris tried to assure him she would see him tomorrow, but he was still crying when the door closed behind him. Oscar held onto Alert's foot, to try to comfort him as they walked back to their building.

Glad that they were already in their own building, Doris and Christine carefully climbed the stairs, eager to settle into their new bed. They joined the line and used the bathroom first. Once they got into bed, Christine asked for a bedtime story. Doris was so full of ideas for the story that she hardly knew where to begin, but before she could even start, Christine was sound asleep. Doris was kind of glad. Their bed was soft and there were three blankets to keep them warm. At eight years old, she didn't understand all of her feelings and thoughts, or the aches in her body from carrying her baby brother all afternoon. She lay in bed waiting for sleep. She needed to sleep.

The big room, with nine other girls, was now dark and quiet, and her thoughts went back to Aunt Jessie's flat in Elizabeth. Sadness came over her as she thought of the empty bed they slept in just last night, and Pappa, alone in their old flat down the street, and Mamma far away in heaven. Her eyes filled with tears, but as she squeezed them out and they fell onto her sheet, she too fell asleep.

As she was waking the next morning, her mind was already racing. She was thinking about their new home, new routines and rules, new responsibilities, new faces and names and the still unknown adventures of a new school. But any awareness of what she had experienced before or what she was facing this Monday morning, were completely forced out of her mind, when she realized that under the warm covers, was an additional feeling of warmth, accompanied by wet.

"Oh No! Christine, Christine, wake up!"

"What?"

"Christine, what have you done!"

"I don't know. What do you mean?"

"You have wet our bed!"

"Oh Doris, I didn't mean to, I don't know what happened. Oh no, what will we do?"

Instinct drove them out of the bed, and standing there in their wet pajamas quickly became too cold for the little girls. They pulled a few dry blankets from the top of the bed and wrapped them around themselves while they thought.

"We need a grown up to tell us what to do," Doris whispered. But there weren't any grown-ups in sight. Doris ventured out into the hall, toward the bathroom. The wooden floor was cold on her bare feet, but that was the least of her problems. Still there were no grown-ups in sight. The *big girls* were already up, as they had responsibilities in the kitchen and dining room, so there was already a long line at the bathroom. At the end of the bathroom line, Doris spotted a familiar face. It was Dottie. Doris knew it wasn't polite to whisper in front of other people, but she over-ruled that obstacle and stood on her tip toes, and whispered through her cupped hands, into Dottie's ear.

"Dottie, my sister wet our bed. What do we do?"

Dottie, not in a position to give up her spot on the line, whispered back into Doris's ear. "It's okay. It happens all the time to someone, here. Go back to your bed, and as soon as I come out of the bathroom, I will come and help you."

Dottie's kindness was more than Doris had hoped for. She went back to Christine who was still standing beside their bed, wrapped in the blanket. "Christine, do you need to go to the bathroom?"

Doris couldn't believe she really did, but her emphatic "YES!" left no question.

Doris instructed her, "Don't tell anyone about this. Keep the blanket wrapped around you and get on the bathroom line." Christine started to walk away, but Doris quickly (and carefully) brought her back to the bed, when she saw the wet drops making a trail behind the cold, sleepy, embarrassed, six year old.

"Here, Christine, give me your underpants." She helped her sister out of her wet pants and tucked them under the top blanket and the wet sheet on the bottom. "Okay," she said, in a very low voice, "now after you go *tissy* wash yourself off good, like Mamma showed us how to wash Alert when we changed his diaper, so you don't smell bad." Then she sent Christine back to the line, and used her own, dry underpants to dry the drops on the floor.

With distant sounds of the toilet repeatedly flushing, Dottie finally walked silently into where Doris was sitting on a dry spot on the bed, waiting.

"Doris, put all of the wet sheets in a pile under your bed, and put the dry blankets on top of the bed, just as if the bed was made-up the normal way. When I finish in the Dining room, there will be a few minutes before I have to catch the bus for school. I will come back and bring the wet things to the laundry for you."

Doris was so embarrassed; what an awful first impression. The girls would probably think it was her - maybe Dottie already thought that. Fortunately the girls in their room were all still asleep, but she guessed it wouldn't be long before they started waking up, so she quickly did what Dottie told her to do.

Dottie's kindness helped them through this crisis. *Soon I will learn where the laundry is, and how to take care of this problem, but I hope it will never happen again,* she thought. This morning, she definitely needed the help. There were already far more new things planned for this day that she would still have to take care of.

"Thank you so much," Doris whispered, and she went right to work. She knew from changing Alert's diapers at home that you don't put the wet things right on the wooden floor. First you put enough dry things to keep the floor from getting wet and smelling like urine.

With Dottie's help, Doris was ready to face the dazed little girl returning from the bathroom. They dressed in the school clothes they had brought from Aunt Jessie's. The matching blue dresses were a little wrinkled from being in the pillowcases, but for today, they would not worry about wrinkles. Both Haukland girls were ready, despite their little secret, long before the bell rang to go for breakfast.

They went downstairs, since they didn't know what else to do. When they had passed the big window on the landing, they noticed that the snow was almost gone, and the sun was shining. They sat together, against the wall, on the bottom step of the big stairway closest to Father Nelson's office. They watched all the other girls scurrying around and running up and down the stairs, like it was as easy as walking on level ground. Doris imagined that soon she too would be able to do that without holding the railing.

Christine was pressed snugly into Doris's side while they were sitting there. Normally, Christine liked to think of herself as very independent and self-confident, but the events of the morning and the uncertainty of the day ahead seemed a little less ominous when she could feel her older sister close to her.

More children came to sit on the steps, and Doris noticed they were all putting on coats and hats. Remembering they would have to go outside once the bell rang, Doris said,

"Christine, you stay here. I'll run up and get our coats and hats, and I'll be right back."

Christine drew in a quick breath, and was about to object to staying there alone, but she caught herself, overriding the insecurity she was feeling at the moment. She sat back and thought hard to convince herself that she was all right and the worst of this day was already over.

With their coats buttoned, and hats and mittens in place, they were prepared when the bell rang for breakfast. The girls jumped off their step and were among the first to make the crossing from their building to the boys building. Again, the big boys were carrying the very big pots, calling out,

"HOT POTS COMING THROUGH!"

This morning, Doris was comfortable that they were not a threat - at least not with those pots in their hands!

A very sleepy Oscar was coming down the steps, dutifully holding the hand of his brother. Unlike Oscar, Alert looked wide awake and ready for fun! When Doris and Christine came in the front door, the boys looked surprised and confused. Quickly their expressions turned into enthusiastic greetings. All four children celebrated. There were hugs and lots of bouncing up and down. Before entering the dining room, Christine and Doris found empty hooks on the wall in the hallway and hung their coats with the mittens in the pockets and the hat in one sleeve.

Doris felt a little sheepish when she first saw Dottie in the dining room, but Dottie gave no hint of knowing their secret. She greeted all of the Haukland children and helped them get settled at the table next to Alert's high chair. The room was again quiet, and the children were waiting for something. Doris guessed it was for the food to come out, but before that happened, Miss Bersager came in and began to talk.

"Good Morning. I hope you are all ready to get back to school this morning! I want to read a verse from Revelation 19, to you. Can anyone tell me where in the Bible the book of Revelation is?" Most of the children raised their hands, and several were waving enthusiastically, hoping to be called.

"Bruce," Miss Bersager said.

Bruce seemed very pleased with himself as he answered,

"It's the last book in the Bible."

"That's right, Bruce. The verse is in chapter 19, and it's verse 7. It says: This is the day that the Lord hath made, let us be glad and rejoice in it."

Miss Bersager spoke on for a minute or two, but Doris was deep in thought. She repeated the verse again to herself, remembering that she had heard her Mamma recite this verse in the morning before they all went off for the day. She even remembered a song her mother taught her that had those words in it.

The pit that she had been feeling in her stomach every time she let herself think about going to a new school seemed to be washed down when she resolved *the Lord made this day, and it is my job to be happy with whatever it brings.*

Her attention was drawn back to Miss Bersager as she finished asking God's blessing on their food and the day, and they all ate their hot oatmeal with brown sugar and warm milk, in silence. Spoons hitting the glass dishes, as they ate their oatmeal, and the helpers walking around the room made the only noise. When the cereal was eaten, the empty bowls were filled with milk for the younger children, and milk with coffee, for the older ones.

Alert readily gave up the "game" he had been playing at mealtime. He happily fed himself anything that he could, and allowed Doris to help him with things that required skillful use of a spoon. Doris was very happy to help him, or Christine, or Oscar and even the other yet-unknown children at their table.

Chapter 8
A New School

After most children had finished eating, Miss Bersager entered the dining room. She announced: "You're Dismissed." Suddenly, the noise was unbelievable! Doris wiped Alert and Oscar's faces, and checked Christine to be sure there was no milk mustache that she would wear on her first day in the new school.

Realizing time would have to teach the boys that their sisters would be back after school, she kissed them and settled them in the little play room in their building.

Most of the children started their walk down the hill, but Doris and Christine returned to their building. Before going to Father Nelson's office, they went back up stairs to use the bathroom. With all the other girls already on their way to school, there was no line. Before long they were back downstairs, sitting on the steps outside the glass doors of Father Nelson's office.

"Are we ready?" Father Nelson asked, sticking his head out one of the doors.

"Yes, Father Nelson," they said together.

Father Nelson went back and got the keys for the

Dodge from his desk. He grabbed his coat from the coat stand just inside the doors, and his hat from on top of the stand. With one hand still working its way into the sleeve, he stepped into the big open room where the girls were buttoning their coats.

"Did you get a good night sleep after your busy day yesterday?" he asked.

The girls looked quickly at each other. *Did Father Nelson know what happened this morning*, they wondered. Before they could say anything, though, Father Nelson continued to talk. "It looks like we'll be getting more snow today. Once you find out which classes you will be in, we'll see if we can get your books and drive back to The Home. You can have your first day in class tomorrow. You will walk to school with some of the older girls, if the snow has stopped."

Father Nelson unlocked the car, and opened the passenger door for Doris and Christine. Once they were settled in the front seat, he closed the door, walked behind the car and got into the driver's seat. The girls didn't say anything out loud, but this was the first time they would ride in a car. They were used to trolleys, busses, and ferries, but had never ridden in a car. It felt funny in their stomachs when they rode down the steep hill toward the main road. Eventually they decided it was fun, but they still said nothing.

In the elementary school office, Father Nelson said: "Miss O'Connor, these two young ladies came to live with us at The Christian Orphan Home, yesterday. This is Christine Haukland. She is six and will have another birthday in two months, and this is Doris Haukland. She is eight and her birthday is in July."

Miss O'Connor reached across her desk and shook hands with each of the girls.

"Welcome to Fort Lee and to Elementary School Number Two. This is a wonderful school, and I'm sure you will be happy here." Pointing to the door they just came through she said, "Why don't you take your coats off and hang them behind the door. We will just do a few little tests to make sure you get in the right classes. Doris, I will give you a little book to read, and then I will ask you write the answers to a few questions. Christine, I will read you a story, and then ask you some questions about the story. Ready?"

"Yes, Miss O'Connor," they responded somewhat shyly.

"Doris, would you please sit in that little room over there and read this short story and answer the questions at the end? There is a pencil on the desk in that room. Christine, I will read to you and have her write some letters and numbers for me. Christine, you can come and sit here right next to my desk."

Father Nelson sat looking at a newspaper, as Miss O'Connor read a story to Christine. When the story was completed, Christine was able to correctly answer every question she was asked. Miss O'Connor read a series of letters and numbers, and watched as Christine skillfully used her left hand to neatly write them on the paper she had been given.

When the testing was completed she said, "Very good, Christine, but you won't be allowed to use your left hand for writing any more. You will have to learn to write with your right hand, now."

Doris found the assignment very easy and she finished the story and answered all of the questions before Christine was even finished. Once Miss O'Connor reviewed Doris's answers, she said, "Doris, you did very well. I know you were in the third grade, in Elizabeth, but here you will go into the second grade, because we want you to have a good foundation, and there may have been some things your old school didn't cover."

With the testing completed and decisions made, Miss O'Connor looked through several lists before she wrote down a teacher's name and classroom number for each of the girls. She was getting ready to bring them into their new classes when Father Nelson addressed his hope of getting their books and driving them back to The Home today.

When Miss O'Connor looked out the window and saw the snow already falling, she said, "That's a very good idea, but before you leave, I'd like the girls to meet their new teachers, and see where the class meets, so they will know where to go tomorrow."

"Excuse me, Miss O'Connor," Doris interrupted, "Could I use the girls room?"

"Certainly, Doris, it's the second door on the right after you leave this room."

Doris closed the bathroom door behind her. Leaning back against it, she slid down, so that she was sitting on her heels. She tightly folded her hands, squeezed her eyes closed, took a breath and whispered: "Jesus, I was disappointed when Miss O'Connor said I will be put back into second grade and when she told Christine that she can't write with her left hand. I want to tell you, that I am not going to be upset or angry or even stay disappointed by these things. I am going to be happy and trust You to be the one who puts Christine and me in just the right classes. It's nice to have You here with me in school, and I want You to know that I'm not just going to pretend I'm okay with this, but I really believe that it will be the best possible thing for us, because You love us."

Doris didn't even say amen. This wasn't the end. It was

just another giant step in learning to trust her Heavenly Father.

Christine whispered to Doris as they walked down the hall, behind Miss O'Connor.

"Doris, I can't write with my right hand, it will be worse than being back in kindergarten!"

"You can do it, Christine, you'll just have to practice," Doris whispered back.

The rooms were large and there were a lot of children in the classes already, but the teachers greeted them warmly and said they looked forward to seeing them tomorrow. The falling snow made it difficult to see very far ahead of the car, and Father Nelson was driving much more slowly than before the snow began. The girls were mostly quiet on their way home, only politely answering questions Father Nelson asked about their old school.

Chapter 9
A New Job

*B*ack at the Home, the girls enjoyed a little time in their bedroom when all the others weren't there. They changed into play clothes and settled into a place near their bed, to play. Just like she had promised, Dottie had taken care of their early morning problem and there was a clean, dry sheet and clean blankets on their bed. They dug their dolls out of the pillowcases under their bed. Forgetting everything else, they thought of nothing but playing dolls the way they had so many times before in their home and at Aunt Jessie's.

The lunch bell wouldn't ring, as all the other children in their building were in school, but Miss Bersager came up stairs and asked, "Would you two like to walk with me to the boys building and have lunch with the Tots?"

Doris and Christine had been so involved in their play that they had forgotten about their brothers. Tucking their dolls back into the pillowcases, they quickly put their coats on, and walked through the deepening snow, to enjoy peanut butter and jelly sandwiches and have another chance to be with their brothers.

A New Job

Oscar was sitting in the dining room, but Alert was still upstairs. Doris and Christine ran up to get him. When they entered the Tots's room, they headed for Alert's crib. An older woman was in the back of the room bathing one of the Tots. When she saw Doris and Christine she called out in a heavy Norwegian accent:

"Is one of you Doris?"

A little taken aback, Doris answered, "Yes, I am."

The woman wrapped the child she was bathing in a towel and walked toward the girls. The child, who was still soaking wet, didn't seem bothered by the drops that were coming from her thick wet curls and running down her face. She was ready to get down and play, and the older woman had to work hard to keep her in her arms. When she reached Doris, the woman continued: "Father Nelson told me that you would be taking care of Alert. I haven't had a chance to change his diaper yet."

Doris understood without being told that the woman wanted her to change his diaper. She had done that many times at home, and although it sometimes made her feel sick to her stomach, she knew it had to be done. But as she did it, Doris wondered; *Why did the Superintendent, Father Nelson, talk about changing Alert's diaper. He had so many other things to do, why would he care about Alert's diaper?*

The woman finished drying the little girl, and got her dressed in play clothes, including shoes and socks, while she called to Doris: "The diapers are on the table behind you and there is a tube of cream in the drawer. The sink is in the back where I was when you came in, and there are wash cloths next to the sink."

"Thanks," Doris called back.

Alert, was standing in the corner of his crib. They greeted each other with big smiles and hugs. He was talking to them with the few words he knew, and reaching out his arms for them to lift him out of the crib.

Doris softly and slowly explained, "First I have to change your diaper, Alert. Please lie still so we can get it done and go see Oscar and have lunch."

Alert was amazingly cooperative. Christine entertained him while Doris went to work.

Doris didn't have trouble finding anything she needed to do the job, and she even knew how to place one of the diapers over the front of him as she was working on the back. Christine was glad to leave the immediate area and run to the back of the room and dampen the washcloth for Doris.

The woman hugged the little girl she had dressed. She gave her a loud kiss on her cheek. "There, you look so pretty" she said.

The woman held the little girl's hand as they walked down the steps.

Once she returned, the woman came and stood next to Doris at Alert's crib. Doris could hear her fast, loud breathing as she stood there observing Doris's work. Finally she had caught her breath enough to speak.

"Well, Father Nelson was right. He told me that you were a very capable young lady, and that you knew how to take care of babies."

The woman paused taking a few deep breaths and blowing them out through her lips.

"I'm sorry," she continued "I haven't introduced myself, I am Miss Flotten. I mostly take care of the Tots. A young lady named Tootsie and several of the older girls that live here help out many times, but when they aren't able to be here, there is just too much for me to do."

Miss Flotten's words and presence were encouraging to Doris, and she was glad to be able to help her.

Doris asked, "Where can I find play clothes for Alert?"

Miss Flotten was delighted to show her where Alert's play clothes were. Although lunch was already being served, Miss Flotten continued to show Doris around the nursery, and tell her where she would find things like soap, towels, and more diapers, if the ones by Alert's crib were all used, and where to put the dirty diapers. Finally Miss Flotten realized she was keeping the children from lunch.

"I'm sorry. You must all be hungry. I am usually in my room here in the back, so if you ever need anything, just come and find me."

The girls finished dressing Alert, and then with one sister on each side, he walked down the steps and ran to his high chair.

They arrived in the dining room just as everyone else was ready to say grace. The prayer they said was a traditional prayer said in Norway, before meals. The Haukland's mother had taught it to them when they were in their home in Elizabeth. "*I Jesu navn gårvi til bords å spise, drikke på ditt ord. Deg, Gud til ære, osstil gavn, Så får vi mat i Jesunavn. Amen.*"

Although she didn't realize it wasn't the same way for everyone, Doris was so comfortable with the Norwegian language, that it was just the same to her to recite the prayer in Norwegian, as it would have been to say, *In Jesus's name to the table we go, To eat and drink according to His word. To God the honor, us the gain, So we have food in Jesus's name, Amen.*

It felt strange in the dining room with just the Tots, but they were together, and she and Christine enjoyed being the oldest kids for just this time. After lunch Alert had to take a nap. Oscar and the other older Tots had to rest on their beds for an hour, so Doris and Christine went back to their room to play with their dolls, and talk about school.

Before long, wet, cold children started coming up the hill. Some were carrying books and many were sliding, either accidentally or on purpose. The snow was beautiful and the very clean, white snow now covered the ground, outlined the branches above them, and was still falling through the air.

Once everyone got home, the children either went downstairs to the playroom, or back outside to play in the snow. Those who chose to be out in the snow rolled a little ball of snow until it became a large ball. Some were having snowball fights and some of them were sliding down the hill using anything they could find, even a piece of cardboard.

After their rest, Alert, Oscar and all the other Tots were brought over to the girls's building, to play. With so many children in the playroom, it seemed small and it was terribly noisy and confusing. The Hauklands all sat in a row, on a bench that was against the wall. Without realizing it, they sat in birth order, Doris, Christine, Oscar then Alert.

Some of the kids tried to be friendly, but it was overwhelming to the newcomers, and none of them was motivated to join in any play. As they sat there, some of the bigger boys stood on the benches and opened the windows that were at the top of the room. They reached out and scooped handfuls of snow, packed it into balls and threw them at the Hauklands! As Doris had bright red hair, she became an easy target. "Red, Red, wet the bed," they chanted, as they threw the snowballs at her and her sister and brothers - inside the playroom!

Doris couldn't believe that anyone would throw wet, cold snow in a house. This just wasn't right, but they were new, and these big boys were not about to listen to her, even if she did say anything. Puddles started to form all over the playroom floor and there didn't seem to be an end to the boys's mischief. Doris decided it was time to get a grownup to stop them. She slipped off the bench and hurried up the steps.

Doris went all the way upstairs to Miss Bersager's room, but she wasn't there. She could not find an adult anywhere in the building! *How are kids supposed to take care of this without a grownup's help,* she wondered.

More and more she was realizing that she was responsible for her siblings. But right now, even her instinct to protect them wasn't enough to get her to walk back down those steps. She could not bear the noise and confusion. Without an adult to intervene on their behalf, she could think of no way to rescue the three defenseless children (or herself) from those boys. They were older and almost twice her size, and their behavior was bolstered and encouraged by each another.

Not one grown up to help, Doris slumped into what was becoming her favorite spot on the bottom step, close to the wall, near Father Nelson's office. It wasn't night, and her pillow wasn't there to cry into, but there was no stopping or delaying the tears. So very alone, she thought to herself as she cried, *Oh Mamma, what can I do?* Her thoughts sought the comfort she would have gotten when she would run to her mother, who always had just the right answer. But when she squeezed out the tears enough to see around her, she was forced back into the moment.

Not knowing exactly why, she thought of the song about the day the Lord made, and her earlier decision to "rejoice and be glad". Thinking back to their home in Elizabeth, she remembered times when Mamma was busy, or when she was sick and needed to sleep. She whispered to herself, *I kept all three of them happy and quiet for hours. Mamma was SO proud of me. I can't stop those big boys from throwing snow at us, or teasing us, but I can ignore them and help my brothers and sister feel happy.* Armed with a fresh attitude and hope, Doris went eagerly down the steps that not ten minutes before, led to a dreaded abyss.

She was so right; her siblings looked so sad and alone as they were still brushing snow off their clothes. Some little girls were busy in one corner, making imaginary dinner, with old pots and pans, or caring for imaginary babies that were pieces of old blankets, wrapped up to look like they were holding dolls. Some kids were jumping rope and singing songs as they jumped.

Doris decided to tell her sister and brothers a story. She spread out an old, worn-out blanket she found on the floor, and gathered her brood around her. Alert, climbed into her lap, Oscar sat next to her on one side, and Christine was on the other side. Doris started out as she had so many times before.

"Once upon a time…" Her mind raced as she tried to think of a story that would be happy, yet calming and comforting.

It was about a little over a year since they had all been together in their flat in Elizabeth, but Doris remembered that Mamma used to tell them stories from the Bible, and she remembered that Oscar loved to hear about Daniel in the Lion's den. As soon as she began the story, she had Oscar's full attention, and she delighted in the smile it brought to his face, when he recognized the story his mother used to tell them. It had been a long time since Doris had heard it, too, but she did her best. A few times Oscar added any parts he thought she had forgotten.

As she spoke, the rest of the room quieted down. Actually, the sound level may not have truly changed, but as far as the Hauklands were concerned, there was no one else in the room.

A New Job

The boys who were teasing so cruelly eventually gave up and went to look for mischief someplace else. One of the children whom Doris recognized as the girl, who slept in the bed next to theirs, wandered over and sat on the corner of their blanket. She had been listening to Doris's story, and now she asked if she could sit on their blanket with them.

"We would love to have you join us," Doris said, and there was no objection from any of the others. The little girl brightened and sat next to Christine. Doris noted that they looked like they were very close in age. By the time Daniel was let out of the den, since the hungry lions were just walking peacefully around him without hurting him, there were even more children who had moved closer to listen to the story.

Realizing she had so many children enjoying the story, Doris decided to make it into a little play.

"Oscar, would you make believe you are Daniel?" she asked, and Alert and Christine and you" (she said to the little girl whose name she didn't know, yet) "could be the lions?"

Oscar liked that idea, so he stood up, puffed his chest out and looked very brave. Doris began the story again. She explained how the king was tricked into punishing Daniel, because of a new law someone made up, just to get Daniel in trouble. When Doris said Daniel would kneel down and pray to God, Oscar got down on his knees and folded his hands together. By now there were even more children watching, so Doris asked if they would like to join hands and make a den for the lions. Enough children held hands, so there was a large circle for Alert, Christine and the other girl to crawl around in. A few others asked if they could be lions, too, so they stepped inside the circle, and crawled around on their hands and knees.

Doris continued the story, and Oscar walked under two of the children's hands, to enter the "den." Doris continued…

"But God shut the mouth of the lions and none of them hurt Daniel. Then the king knew that Daniel's God was so great that he could even keep the hungry lions from hurting Daniel."

The story ended just before the dinner bell rang and everyone headed for the narrow dark staircase, at the same time. A few of the children stopped and asked Doris if she would tell them another story tomorrow. Doris felt so grown up.

Upstairs, near the front door, all of the children were crowded together around the coat hooks, getting ready to walk back to the brick building. Once Christine, Oscar and Alert were ready, Doris found herself helping a few of the smaller children with their coats.

The snow was a little too deep for Alert to walk through, so Doris carried him. Oscar was struggling, but he was able to get through it, and actually seemed to enjoy the challenge, and the few flops he made into the soft snow.

Before the blessing, Miss Johnson (the older boys's nurse) said, "Make sure you get all of your homework done tonight, so if school is cancelled because of the snow, tomorrow, you'll be able to play in the snow, and if it is not cancelled, you will be ready for school."

The kids cheered at the hope of no school tomorrow, then all the children joined in saying "*I Jesu navn går vi til bords å spise, drikke på ditt ord. Deg, Gud til ære, oss til gavn, Så får vi mat i Jesu navn. Amen.*"

Doris and Christine didn't cheer, but they also tried not to show their disappointment. They both liked school in Elizabeth, and now they were ready to get started in their new classes. Besides, so far the snow hadn't been a lot of fun to any of them except, maybe a little, for Oscar.

A New Job

Between feeding Alert and herself, Doris watched the children sending signs to each other and tried to figure out the letters. The quiet was nice after the noisy playroom. Whatever the signs meant, she was glad for them.

Chapter 10
A Big Sister For A Big Sister

*W*henever Dottie passed their table bringing things in and out of the kitchen, she always smiled at the Hauklands. After Miss Johnson came back and said everyone was dismissed, and most of the kids stampeded toward the door, Dottie stopped to speak with Doris.

"Doris, would you be able to meet me at 6:30 at the bottom of the steps in our building?"

"Sure," Doris replied quickly, then, before Dottie was off to the kitchen again, she added "Thank you, Dottie."

Doris didn't need to say anything more. Dottie knew what she was thanking her for, and called over her shoulder,

"You're welcome, Doris."

Since it was almost five o'clock, Doris decided that she and Christine should just stay in the boys's building until their bedtime, then she would get Christine settled in their room before she met Dottie downstairs.

In the boys's playroom, Oscar's favorite toy seemed to be a wooden truck. He ran it back and forth on the floor, stopping at several places as if he was making a delivery or picking something up. Alert liked playing with blocks. He piled them up until they fell, then he giggled and started over. If someone would stack them up for him, it was his delight to knock every one down!

When Alert started to rub his eyes and yawn, Doris brought him to his room and got him ready for bed. She changed him into his pajamas, and just like her mother had taught her to do for their babies at home, she put on lots of cream and two extra diapers underneath his rubber pants.

Doris noticed a nipple that had cotton stuffed inside it, in his crib. It was a homemade pacifier. Mamma always let the babies use a pacifier when they were going to sleep, so she handed the little nipple to Alert. He quickly popped it into his mouth, and began sucking it. Doris didn't say anything, but she thought he looked too old to still use a pacifier.

Not far from his bed, there was a rocking chair. Alert had grown a lot while he was with their Tante Ulla. He really filled Doris's little lap, but they were both happy to sit and rock. Doris hummed "Jesus Loves Me This I Know" which is what their Mamma would have done. She could feel his body relax and get heavier.

Realizing she was unable to place him down into the crib once he was completely asleep, she put him into his crib while he was almost asleep, but still awake enough to lay himself down. It worked well, but when she leaned over the rail to give him a kiss, she almost fell in. She caught herself, and started to giggle, but he didn't notice, his eyes were peacefully closed.

Christine and Oscar were still playing in the playroom. Doris challenged Oscar: "How fast can you take your play clothes off and put your pajama's on?" Oscar, always ready for a challenge, ran from the playroom, reached under his covers for his pajamas, and started to pull at his shoes and socks. He really was quick.

Christine straightened his socks and clothes out while Doris walked him to the bathroom, then they tucked him into his bed. It had been a long time since they were all together at bedtime.

Doris asked, "Would you like me to tell you a bedtime story?"

"Yes," he answered. "Tell me a story about our family."

Doris smiled and told him a homemade story about four children who lived with many, many other children in two big houses - one for the girls and one for the boys. She told of them all being together to eat and play and grow big and strong, and live happily ever after. Oscar seemed to relax, he smiled at Doris and Christine, letting them know without interrupting, that he knew all four of those children, and he liked the story. Once all of the other Tots were ready for bed, Miss Flotten came in to say their prayers with them. Miss Flotten didn't seem to notice that Alert, who was usually forced to join in, was already sound asleep in his crib. Doris and Christine watched, and then joined in as each of the Tots (including Oscar) got on his or her knees beside their bed and with elbows resting on their beds, folded their hands, closed their eyes and said: "Now I lay me down to sleep. I pray the Lord my soul to keep. If I should die before I wake, I pray the Lord my soul to take. Amen." Then they each crawled into their beds. Alert never stirred. The girls kissed Oscar good night and started toward the front door.

Miss Flotten met them in the hallway. By now she had noticed that Alert was already asleep and that they had helped both Oscar and Alert get ready for bed.

"Doris, thank you so much. It is so nice that you and Christine helped your brothers and me. I'm so glad you are here with them. They both seem so much happier today!"

Even the cold snow didn't dampen the warm, happy feeling Doris had. She and Christine were the only ones walking on the little road between the buildings. It was dark, except for the lights coming from the buildings, but they were not afraid. The snow was still falling steadily. The air was crisp. Neither of the girls spoke, enjoying the perfect silence.

The big, warm house felt good, too. It was almost 6:30, so Doris walked Christine up to their bed and settled her there before going back downstairs to meet Dottie. Doris was impressed with her own ability to go down the steps without holding the rail. She was still very slow and cautious, but she was already making progress! Well, she thought she was doing well, until she turned and watched Dottie come flying down without looking or holding the rail!

"Wow!" Doris said, before she realized the word was out of her mouth.

"What?" asked Dottie.

"You're so fast on the steps."

"Oh that's nothing; you'll be doing that before you know it! I wanted to show you the laundry room. Grab your coat. Usually, none of the Home kids ever bring laundry there, or get clean laundry from there, unless that's their job, on laundry day. I was happy to be able to help you and Christine this morning. You can always ask one of the nurses, Miss Flotten, Miss Johnson or Miss Bersager, if you have an unusual problem. I just thought you'd like to get to know more about your new Home."

Walking next to Dottie out in the cold, snowy night, Doris thought *I really like being the big sister, but it would be fun to pretend that Dottie is my big sister.* Of course, she wouldn't say anything about that to Dottie, not tonight. Tonight was the time to be grown-up, herself.

"Dottie, how long have you lived here?" asked Doris.

"I've lived here since I was five, and now I'm twelve and a half."

"I guess that's why you know everything," replied Doris.

"Oh, I don't know everything, but I know where most things are, and I know what kids feel like when they first get here. I remember when I first came here, and I needed someone to tell me where everything was. When I can help anyone feel more comfortable, I like to do that."

"I know you sure helped Christine and me feel a lot better, already!"

"Thanks, Doris. I know you miss being with your parents, but this is a really wonderful place to live. I have made so many good friends here. There is a lot of work to do, but everyone pitches in, and a lot of time the work is really fun, at the same time."

"That sounds nice, Dottie. I like to work. You're right about missing my parents. That's the hardest thing, but before my mother died, she asked me to keep the family together. For a long time, Alert and Oscar have been living with one of our Aunts and Christine and I have been living with a different Aunt, and we only got to visit them once, on Easter, before they came to the Home. Now that Christine and I are here with the boys, well, it just feels better than when we were so far apart."

This time, they didn't go up the narrow cement steps on the side of the brick building, they went around to the side facing the Hudson River. That was really the front of the building. They went past a large brick staircase until they got to a doorway into the ground floor. As Dottie pulled the door open, although Doris didn't say it out loud, she remembered that the strong smell of bleach that wafted over her, was the reason she hated laundry day in their flat in Elizabeth.

The room was cold and dimly lit by one exposed bulb in the center of the ceiling. Puddles remained on the floor around the washing machines and under the sheets and towels remaining on the clotheslines. The lines were strung neatly back and forth across one side of the room making long, neat rows. Doris thought *this would be a fun place to play tag.* It hadn't been very long since the workers had gone home, yet as she walked past the wet sheets, they felt cold and stiff against her skin, almost as if they could be starting to freeze. The only sound was the steady drip from the towels.

On the far side of the room there was a stove with two large pots resting on it, a sink and two washing machines. The washers were very large copper-colored tanks with wooden cylinders inside them, motors under them on a stand, and rollers attached to the top. The wooden cylinders had lots of holes in them.

Dottie explained how the laundry was done, as if she was giving a tour to a class on a field trip. "The workers heat water on the stove, then pour it into the tub, add soap and bleach, then place the dirty laundry which is separated into dark or white, into the cylinders. Then a motor makes the cylinders turn around and around to wash the clothes. The holes let the water and soap move in and out of the clothes. Next the heavy, soaking wet, soapy things are fed into these two round, rubber rollers that are fixed on the top of the washing tubs. The dirty, soapy water gets squeezed back into the tubs, and the squeezed laundry is placed in a basket. Then the dirty water is drained out and the tubs are rinsed. Next, more heated water is poured into the tubs, but no more soap is added, and all the wet clothes in the basket go back into the tubs to be rinsed. After the rinse, the clothes again get put through the ringers or into this white machine, which is called an extractor. It spins very fast and takes even more of the water out, so the laundry dries more quickly once it is hung on the clotheslines. When the weather is warm, the laundry is hung on lines, outside."

In the middle of the room was a large table, that had several piles of neatly folded clothes at one end, and one wall was covered with shelves for the clean laundry to be kept once it was ready to be used again. Under the only window in the room, there was a white machine with a big round cloth-covered roll, with what looked like burn marks on it. It had a rounded top that was above the roll, which was curved in a way that would fit snugly, over the roll.

Doris walked over to examine this unfamiliar machine, and before she realized it might be a foolish question, she asked, "What's this, Dottie?"

"That's called a mangle. It takes the wrinkles out of the sheets and towels, and some of the clothes.

Seeing that Doris was intent on learning everything about her new home, Dottie continued. "You won't have to learn how to use any of these machines. Grown ups come from the town, and do all the laundry. On Saturday someone will bring one of those big baskets on wheels, to each building," she said, pointing to two carts next to the table in the middle of the room, "and collect all the dirty laundry."

"When you get older," Dottie added, "you'll learn how to darn socks. Monday is wash day, so on Tuesday, you will take a big pile of socks, darn the holes, then bring them back to be handed out the following week."

"I already know how to darn socks," Doris said.

"That's great; there are a *lot* of socks that get new holes each week! Well, that's all there is to know about the laundry, for now," Dottie said.

"Okay," said Doris, comfortable that she had a good understanding of the laundry room.

As they left the brick building, Dottie continued. "Every Saturday, you will get a clean sheet for your bed, and a clean set of clothes, underwear, sox and pajamas will be put on your bed. You keep the top sheet on your bed, but now it is the bottom sheet, and you put the clean sheet on the top, then the blankets go next. Saturday night is bath night, so after your bath you start to use your clean clothes. The basket with wheels will be rolled over in front of our building, and everyone will put her dirty sheet and clothes in that basket. You won't have to remember this, you can just watch everyone else and do the same thing."

Dottie took a deep breath smelling the clean, fresh air, and they agreed that the snow seemed to be letting up. Then Dottie said, "In the summer, when we go to West Park, you'll have to wash any wet sheets yourself and then hang them on a line outside, to dry. Then you put them back on your bed at night."

"What do you mean when we go to West Park, Dottie?" Doris asked.

"Oh you don't know about that? Once school is out, busses take us all to a wonderful place in the country, kind of like going to camp. We stay there until school starts again in September. There is a creek for us to swim in and lots of space to play outside. There are lots of trees and grass and the air smells so clean - it's just wonderful there."

Doris was silent. The things Dottie was saying, the excitement in her voice and the way she was smiling and moving her arms like she was swimming, should have made this West Park place sound appealing. But instead, the sudden tightness in her stomach made Doris want to put her fingers in her ears, so she didn't hear any more of what Dottie was describing. She didn't like the thought of leaving Fort Lee for the summer. This already felt like the country compared to Elizabeth. She definitely didn't want to be any further away from where her Aunts and Uncles lived, or any further away from Pappa. She thought about how long it took them to get to Fort Lee from their home in Elizabeth and she began to wonder how Pappa would be able to get to this "camp" to visit them. Right now, she already had so many other things to think about, so she decided not to think about camp until the weather got warmer.

When they got back to their building, Dottie said, "So that's it. Did I forget to tell you anything about laundry?"

"No," said Doris. "Thanks, Dottie. Christine hasn't wet the bed since she was three years old. I guess it's just that everything is so new to her. I hope it won't happen again."

"Oh good," said Dottie, "the long lines for the bathroom are especially hard for the little girls. Well, I've got to get to my homework in case we have school tomorrow, so let's head back upstairs. Maybe tomorrow I can show you some of the letters we make with our fingers, while we're in the dining room."

"I'd love that, thanks!" said Doris.

Dottie didn't show off on the way up the big steps. She didn't hold onto the rail, but she didn't run up two steps at a time, like Doris had seen some of the other girls do. Doris thought, *that was nice of her. She really would be a great big sister.*

Christine was almost asleep, so Doris quickly convinced her to make one last trip to the bathroom before she was too deep into sleep to walk all the way down the hall. There was no line, so it was quick. When she returned, she climbed into the bed, and didn't even have the time to ask for a story before she was asleep.

It was still early, but Doris was tired, too. Some of the other younger girls were also already sleeping. Doris put on her pajamas, and lay down next to Christine. Her eyes closed as soon as her head rested on the bed, but sleep didn't come right away. Doris thought about school. She loved going to school in Elizabeth. Each day they learned something new, and the teacher always told her mother that Doris was one of the first children to understand the new material. Her teacher here would be Miss Baker, and Doris hoped that she would like her, and that she would get good grades here, too. Suddenly her thoughts were interrupted by a tiny, strange, yet familiar sound in the room.

The sound was disturbing to Doris. She would have to decide whether the right choice would be to ignore it and pretend she was asleep, or to try to address it. She opened her eyes to see where this muffled expression of sadness was coming from. The room was now gently lit by the white light of the moon, reflecting off the snow, and Doris was able to see that the girl who was crying, was the same one who had joined them earlier while she was telling the story in the playroom.

The snow had stopped falling. There would be school again tomorrow. The thought of getting down that snow-covered hill with her schoolbooks and her sister quickly ran through her mind, but then her thoughts returned to the girl in the next bed. Doris could see the small hump beneath the blankets in the bed next to theirs, jerking up and down.

Many nights while she was at Aunt Jessie's house, when everyone else was asleep, Doris would cry. She really missed her mother, and especially once she knew her mother wouldn't be coming home again. No one had heard her, and no one came to comfort her. Doris remembered that she was glad no one heard her cry. Even though it made her eyes puffy and her ribs hurt in the morning, it just made her feel better inside. Maybe it was best to pretend she didn't hear anything, and just try to include this little girl as part of their family during the day.

Doris decided that if the sobbing didn't stop in a few minutes, she would get up and make sure the girl was okay. She started counting to herself, trying to keep track of the time, but before she reached one hundred, the little hump stretched out, her head turned to the side, and all was quiet. That was the last Doris remembered of her first full day at the Home.

Chapter 11
Good Morning Miss Baker – Good Afternoon Miss Goodman

In the morning, Doris felt rested - and dry! What a perfect way to start this day!

"Quick, Christine! It's morning, and there's no one on line for the bathroom!"

"Are you sure it's morning, Doris?" Christine answered, trying to force her eyes open.

"Yes it is, and it isn't snowing any more, so we'll probably get to go to school today!"

"Okay," Christine said, as she flung back the covers and headed for the bathroom. Once both sisters were dressed, Doris noticed the little girl in the next bed struggling to tie the sash behind her dress.

"Can I help you?" Doris asked.

"Oh please," the little girl answered.

Doris noticed tears in the little girl's eyes when she went over to help. "My name is Doris and this is my sister, Christine. Christine is six, how old are you?"

"I'm six too!" the little girl answered. A smile now started on her face, and the tears in her eyes disappeared as she ran her sleeve across her eyes. "My name is Nancy. I just came here last week, and I don't know anybody here. Today I have to start school, and I'm so scared. Father Nelson said I could go with three older girls, but I don't know who they are!"

Doris, who was an expert at tying, made a perfect bow behind Nancy's back. "Don't worry," she told Nancy. "We are supposed to go to school with three older girls, too, so we will probably be together. Maybe Christine will be in the same class as you are." This seemed to be encouraging to Nancy, and she smiled shyly at Christine. The bell sounded and the three new girls knew it was time to walk through the snow, to get their breakfast.

At the bottom of the steps, underneath the coat hooks; there were rows of red rubber boots. Each of the girls was trying to pick a pair that would fit over her shoes. The three new girls went to work, and before long they were all pulling the red rubber boots up over their shoes, buttoning their coats and heading out in the snow.

The sun was bright, shining off the snow, and the snow that lined the branches was melting and dripping down on the road. *Maybe after breakfast most of the snow would be gone from the road and it wouldn't be so hard to get down that steep hill*, Doris thought.

Stepping into the big brick house, the noise of happy children talking loudly hit their ears as the smell of maple syrup reached their noses. Pancakes! That made this day even more special! Oscar and Alert called to their sisters and Alert kicked his feet against the high chair, in excitement, as the girls came into the dining room.

Doris moved an empty chair from the next table, and made a place for Nancy to join their family. As the Hauklands hugged each other, Doris introduced her brothers to Nancy, and told her that she and Christine had been separated from their brothers for over a year. They all settled into their places. This morning, Father Nelson would lead them in the announcements, the morning devotions and the blessing on the food.

"I guess you all know by now that there will be school today, even though there is quite a bit of snow on the ground. The girls have already gotten boots, and the boys's boots will be ready, in the hallway outside the dining room, after breakfast. This morning, I'd like to read to you from First Thessalonians, chapter five, verses 16, 17 and 18.

"Rejoice evermore.

Pray without ceasing.

In every thing give thanks: for this is the will of God in Christ Jesus concerning you."

"Who knows another way to say rejoice?"

One of the bigger girls, who was wearing a red plaid dress, raised her hand and said in a loud, clear voice, "Be happy."

"Great," said Father Nelson. "Anybody know what it means to do something without ceasing?"

The same girl answered, "Without stopping."

"Right. Then, when the next verse says "in everything give thanks," do you think that it means that if everything is going well for you, to say thank you to God, or do you think it means that we should be thankful even when some things aren't going our way? Maybe someone else could answer this one."

A different older girl raised her hand. She looked like she really wanted to answer, but it seemed hard for her to get her words out. Even with everyone else quiet, it was hard to hear what she said: "I think it means that even when things aren't going the way we'd like them to, we should remember that God may have a reason for that, and we should be able to say thank you, even if it doesn't feel right at the moment."

"Great answer, Mildred," said Father Nelson. With that he looked down, closed his eyes and said, "Thank You, Lord for this beautiful new day. Help us to remember to trust you with everything in our lives. Please bless this food to our bodies and us to your service. Amen."

Once he left the room, there were only quiet voices, the sounds of dishes and utensils, and little fingers wiggling, sending messages back and forth across the room.

The soft, sweet pancakes and cold milk were brought out and the Haukland children, and their new friend, Nancy, enjoyed every bite. Alert loved feeding himself the pancakes, but Doris wished she had a garden hose to wash him off afterward.

Father Nelson returned and announced that the children were dismissed. Just as they did after every meal, the bigger boys almost trampled anyone in their way as they charged through the doorway. Doris wondered why they had to be so rough and noisy, but decided she'd just get used to it.

While helping Alert out of his high chair, keeping him as far from her school dress as she could, she noticed that he also needed a clean diaper. On her way upstairs, she passed Miss Flotten who was coming down. Miss Flotten said, "Good Morning, Doris, I hope you will find everything you need this morning. I left a clean diaper and a wash cloth in Alert's crib so you don't have to go looking for anything since this is your first full day of school."

"Thank you, Miss Flotten."

Alert had been changed and dressed earlier this morning. Now she would only need to clean him and change his diaper. Now Doris realized it would be better and more helpful to Miss Flotten if she would get Alert ready for the day, before she went to school, instead of having Miss Flotten or one of her other helpers wash and dress her brother. She determined that this would be her first job, every morning.

But now, Doris had to work quickly and carefully, so she wouldn't get her school clothes soiled or make the others she was to walk to school with, late. Alert seemed to sense the seriousness of the situation, and he was very cooperative. Doris remembered everything Miss Flotten had shown her yesterday, but since she hadn't planned on caring for Alert before school, she was glad the diaper and washcloth were laid out on his crib. As she cleaned him up, she played a game to keep him calm and help him learn the names of different parts of his body.

"Alert, where is your nose?" Alert loved this game and he was quite good at it.

"Nos," he said as he put his little finger on his nose.

"That's right," said Doris. "And where is your hair?"

Putting both hands on top of his head, catching fists-full of blond curls, he said, "Air."

His little white teeth were all showing as he smiled broadly, Doris asked, "Where are your teeth?"

Alert put his top and bottom teeth together, rested his index finger against his front teeth and proudly said, through his clenched ones, "Teef!"

With three correct answers for three tries, she said, "That's terrific, Alert! Good job!" She gave him a quick tickle on both sides of his belly, pulled up his pants and stood him up just inside his crib rail. Before lifting him out, Doris quickly ran a brush through Alerts blond curls and then brought her fresh-smelling baby brother to the play area, where Oscar, Christine and Nancy were waiting.

Saying goodbye to the boys to go to school was a little hard, but she knew it would only be for a few hours, and though she wasn't sure Alert understood everything she was saying to him, she knew Oscar did, so she explained that they would be back after school, and then they could play again. The girls kissed Oscar and Alert goodbye and Oscar distracted Alert with the toys while Doris, Christine and Nancy left.

As they walked back to their building to meet the three bigger girls who would show them the way to their new school, Doris thought about what Father Nelson read before breakfast. Being with the boys was so good, and now they had a friend, too.

Watching over her brothers and sister was something that would have helped her Mamma, if she were still alive. Although they would have to wait until the Sunday after this coming one to see Pappa again, at least most of the time, the children were together.

Feeling like it was easy to say, Doris whispered, "*Thank You, Lord.*" Her happy heart made her feel like skipping. So even with her loose fitting, flimsy red rubber boots slipping partly off and on with each step, Doris skipped all the way back to the big stone building.

The three bigger girls were standing in front of the building. They waited for Doris, Christine and Nancy to get their books, and take off their rubber boots, since most of the snow on the street had already melted. Except for when they had to cross the big streets, they didn't even seem to remember the younger girls were trailing behind them. The girls showed them where they would meet after school, then the big girls continued to walk a little further, to the middle school.

The elementary school building was warm, and the familiar school sounds and smells were comforting to Doris. Before she looked for her own room, she went to the office to see where Nancy should go. The two six year olds were to report to the same room. They smiled at each other and walked the rest of the way holding hands.

"When school is over, we'll meet the older girls right here. Don't forget!" Doris said. She remembered exactly where her classroom was, from her introduction on Monday, and was able to walk right to it without getting lost.

Miss Baker was standing by the door when Doris arrived. She said "Welcome, Doris. We're very happy to have you join our class. I have fixed this desk just for you. Please let me know if you have any trouble seeing the chalk board from your seat."

She made Doris feel even more special, by pinning a nametag on her dress, just under her right shoulder. It simply said DORIS.

"Thank you, Miss Baker," Doris said as she fit her books into the desk, and sat quietly waiting for her new school day to begin. Miss Baker had put two new pencils with sharp points in the groove at the top of the desk, and there was already some black ink in the inkwell up in the corner. Doris knew from her old school that when it was time to practice penmanship with the ink, the teacher would give out the pens, and everyone had to be very careful how they used the ink, because it made such a mess.

When almost all the seats were filled, Miss Baker closed the door and said, "Good Morning, class. Would you all stand for the pledge of allegiance to our flag?"

Doris was so happy. This was just like her class in Elizabeth! She knew every word, and spoke loud enough that Miss Baker was sure to know she did. They also sang "The Star Spangled Banner," then Miss Baker said a prayer.

Once everyone was in his or her seat, Miss Baker said, "I would like you all to meet our new classmate. This is

Doris Haukland. She just moved to Fort Lee from Elizabeth NJ." Miss Baker didn't say anything more about Doris, or her family. Doris wondered, *was it because she didn't know more or that she didn't want to take any more time from their studies or...*

The reason wasn't important Doris took a deep breath. At least for now, Doris didn't want the others in her class to know that her mother had died, or that her father lived in Brooklyn and he was not very healthy, or that she now lived in an orphan home where her brothers were in a different building, and she and her sister slept in a room with nine other girls and they ate in a dining room with about seventy other children. Right now, she just wanted to be one of the girls in Miss Baker's second grade class. She wanted to get good grades so her teacher and her Pappa would be proud of her, and she wanted to learn. Doris wanted to learn enough to some day be a nurse... or a dancer. Which ever it would be, she wanted to learn everything she could.

Miss Baker handed out sheets of paper with math problems. As she placed the test on Doris's desk she said. "I know you weren't here when we learned this material, but do the best you can, and I won't give you a bad grade if you don't get the answers right."

Doris was a little nervous, but when she looked at the problems, she thought *I know exactly how to do these problems,* and she went right to work. She worked quickly, and seemed to finish before the others. When Doris looked up, Miss Baker walked over to her desk. The expression on Doris's face told Miss Baker that Doris wasn't having difficulty with the work.

"Have you finished already, Doris?"

"Yes, Miss Baker."

"Did you already learn this at your last school?"

"Yes, Miss Baker."

"While the other children finish their math, I will give you a different test on grammar and punctuation."

When Miss Baker collected the other children's math papers, Doris was still busy on the English paper. Miss Baker said nothing to Doris, or to the rest of the class, she just nodded to Doris, and her gestures let Doris know that Miss Baker wanted her to finish what she was doing, instead of paying attention to what the rest of the class was doing next.

When she was finished with the paper, Doris put down her pencil, and joined the rest of the class. When the bell rang for lunch, Doris placed the English paper on Miss Baker's desk as she walked past, and she and Miss Baker smiled at each other, knowingly.

After lunch, Miss Baker asked Doris if she could talk to her in the hallway, while the others were working on their next project. Doris moved toward the door, wondering if Miss Baker was upset with her. Miss Baker closed the door behind them, so the others wouldn't be distracted from their work.

"Doris," she said, "I love having you in my class, but I think that you really belong in the third grade, instead of the second grade."

Doris felt relieved that Miss Baker wasn't angry with her.

Miss Baker continued, "During lunch, I spoke with the Principal and with Miss Goodman, who is the third grade teacher. We have decided to move you into Miss Goodman's class, right away. Will that be all right with you?"

"I'm sorry I won't be in your class any more. I liked having you for my teacher," Doris said to Miss Baker.

"Oh thank you, Doris. I was looking forward to having you in my class, but I think this will be a lot better for you.

Miss Goodman is a very good teacher, and I think you will like her very much."

"Yes, Miss Baker," Doris said, as they went back into the class.

Doris took her coat and went with Miss Baker to meet Miss Goodman.

Miss Goodman left her class and joined them in the hall. Miss Baker introduced them, then she returned to her class. Miss Goodman called, "Thank you," to Miss Baker, and then she said, "It's nice to meet you, Doris. Welcome to our class! You will have the seat at the end of the row right next to the window. I have put your new books on the desk. We are up to chapter fifteen - a little more than half way through the book. I won't expect you to finish the lessons you have missed, but if you want to look them over, at home, it may be helpful. The answers to all the questions at the end of each chapter are in the back of the book, so you can be sure that you really understand the work. I won't give you a grade on them, since you weren't here to have the lessons explained in class."

"Okay, Miss Goodman," Doris responded, "Thank you."

She was still wearing the nametag Miss Baker had put on her dress. Miss Goodman had her stand, only briefly, in front of the class, to introduce her. It was a little awkward to start another new class in the middle of the day, but Doris did her best to quietly fit in.

This is a lot harder, Doris thought, as Miss Goodman put the math problems on the board. *I hope, I'll be able to understand what she is doing. Maybe I'll have to ask Dottie to help me, if I can't figure it out on my own.*

Christine was a little cranky and was whining about having to carry her own books. But when she saw Nancy carrying the same books and not complaining at all, she admitted to herself that she really could manage them, if Nancy could. The rest of the trip home, went fine. They followed the bigger girls, and kept up with them. The snow had all melted and the sidewalks and roads were dry.

That evening, after she finished her homework, Doris began at the beginning of her new math book. She worked out every problem and checked the answers in the back of the book, for the first two chapters, and was starting on the third, before she fell asleep with the book next to her in the bed. Before the following Monday, Doris had caught up to the rest of the class in math, without needing to ask her secret big sister to help. Now she would be able to concentrate on English and spelling.

Chapter 12

The Good, The Bad And The Wrinkled

She didn't know why, but the next few mornings, Doris woke up before every one else in her room. She slipped from her bed, being careful to keep the cold from sneaking under the blankets and waking Christine. The bare wooden floors made each step feel like a shock, and it was hard to rest her feet on the clean white tiles on the bathroom floor because that felt even colder than the wood. But even cold feet couldn't dampen her enthusiasm for beginning a new day.

As she passed the East-facing windows, she confirmed the approaching morning by the light beginning to show through the tops of the Manhattan skyscrapers in the distance, and she stretched and whispered, *Good Morning, Lord. Thank you for bringing Christine and me here with Oscar and Alert.*

She had decided that every morning, regardless of whether it was a school day or a Saturday or Sunday, she would wear her play clothes until after breakfast, just in case her clothes got wet or soiled while she was busy with her brothers.

The Good, The Bad And The Wrinkled

With her coat over her play clothes, her scarf over her head and wrapped around her neck, and her hands tucked in her pockets, she walked through the cold, dimly lit morning to the brick building. Oscar was still asleep, but even after just a few days of this routine, Alert was standing in the corner of his crib waiting for Doris when she arrived.

Doris loved the feeling of his warm body against hers and the tickle of his silky hair against her face as he pushed his head into her neck and shoulder. Fortunately, the Tots's room was warmer than the girls rooms in the big stone house, so it wasn't such a shock to Alert when she took off his wet diaper.

He was the first of the Tots to get washed up and dressed. Once he was clean and dry, he was happy to go back into his crib with a toy, and play while he waited for his brother to be ready to go to the playroom with him. Oscar needed very little help once she woke him and laid out his clothes. Doris got so fast at getting her brothers ready, that she soon began helping the other Tots, as well. When each one was dressed and in the playroom waiting for breakfast, she would straighten up the Tots's room, and make all of their beds and cribs.

Tootsie who was Miss Flotten's helper was so pleased with all that Doris did to help her, that she gave Doris the nickname Dukken.[3] This meant doll, in Norwegian. Being called a doll embarrassed Doris, a little, but she loved helping Miss Flotten, Tootsie and the older girls with the Tots, so she didn't tell anyone how embarrassed she was by the nickname.

Waking up on their first Saturday morning was like getting a big box all wrapped in pretty paper that you

3 Dukken (pronounced like Dook-en is the Norwegian word for Doll

have to wait to open. Doris was so eager to find out what her cleaning job was going to be, and when she would get the pile of new clothes and the fresh sheet Dottie had told her would be put on her bed. She thought, *if they read a list of what each kid is going to do, at breakfast, it would take all morning!* It had been fun to go to school this week, but this Saturday morning was especially exciting for her.

Since Doris was already in the brick building when it was time for breakfast, Christine walked over with Nancy. They were becoming good friends. Nancy told Christine that her mother, father and older sister had died in a car crash, just after Christmas. She had been at her Aunt's house, playing with her cousins at the time of the accident. Her Aunt had too many children to keep Nancy, but she promised they would always be together for holidays.

Christine told Nancy that their mother got sick and went to the hospital and died while she was there. The little girls decided that maybe their mothers would be friends in heaven, like they were, at the Home. Doris was glad that Christine had a friend her age, and it made her happy that Nancy wasn't crying any more, when she went to bed.

With everyone gathered in the dining room, Miss Flotten announced that the new list of chores for each building would be posted near the staircase. Doris wanted to jump up right then and go check the list to find her name. She calmed herself down, thinking *at least now I know how I will find out.*

Miss Flotten opened her Bible, and held it very close to her face when she read: "In Proverbs three, the Lord is saying: "My son, forget not my law; but let thine heart keep my commandments: For length of days, and long life, and peace, shall they add to thee. Let not mercy and truth forsake thee: bind them about thy neck; write them upon thine heart: So shalt thou find favour and good understanding in the sight of God and man. Trust in the LORD with all thine heart; and lean not unto thine own understanding. In all thy ways acknowledge Him, and he shall direct thy paths. Be not wise in thine own eyes: fear the LORD, and depart from evil."

Miss Flotten continued: "I am going to read verses five and six again and I would like someone to try to put these verses in his or her own words. Ready? "Trust in the LORD with all thine heart; and lean not unto thine own understanding. In all thy ways acknowledge Him, and He shall direct thy paths."

It took a while for anyone to answer. Finally, a boy raised his hand.

"Thank you for being willing to try this difficult job," Miss Flotten said.

The boy smiled and seemed to relax a little, and then he said, "If you don't know what to do, then pray about it and God will help you."

"Thank you, Harold that was a very good answer. Let's try to remember this when we face difficult things today. Let's pray: Thank you, Lord, for always being with us and directing our paths. Please bless this food to our bodies and us to your service. Amen."

After breakfast, even though it wasn't a school day, Doris settled the boys in the play- room. She gave a quick check to be sure Alert didn't need a clean diaper before kissing them goodbye then she ran back to her building for her first Saturday adventure.

This was a BIG house, and Doris wanted to do her part to keep it clean and neat. As soon as she entered the building she looked for the list. There it was, stuck to a piece of cork on the wall near the steps. She wondered why she never noticed that cork before, but she ran her finger down the list until she found her name. "Doris Haukland - straighten up the play room, dust the shelves and sweep the floor." She was ready to head right down stairs when it caught her eye that there were three other names just under hers that said the same thing. She was to share this job with Christine, Nancy and a girl named Hazel.

Doris had no idea who Hazel might be, and she was a little concerned about doing this important job with someone she didn't even know, but she would try to be kind and work together.

Doris didn't go up stairs - even to see if her new clothes had arrived. The playroom occupied her attention, completely. This was the sixth time she had gone down the dark narrow stairway off to the right, between the front door and the three wide, wooden steps that went into the big entry room.

This time, though, it was HER playroom. She had the rest of the morning and the help of three other girls to make it into the best ever! The room had a slightly musty smell, but that was all right. The mess was overwhelming to Christine and Nancy who were sitting on the bench that lined the wall, waiting for Doris, or anyone who would either get them out of there, or give them an idea of what to do. *Where was Hazel*, Doris wondered? As she scanned the room, and walked around in it, having to clear many obstacles before she could see the floor, a plan was forming in her mind.

Before she could issue directions to Nancy and Christine, Miss Bersager, and a thin girl with very curly light brown hair, who Doris immediately decided was at least 9 years old, came through the doorway.

"Hazel, these are the new girls, Doris, Christine and Nancy," Miss Bersager said, indicating each girl by reaching her hand out in their direction. "You will all be working together in the play room, this morning. Do any of you have any questions before I go back upstairs?"

Although Hazel looked like she was at least 9 years old, she seemed to be uncomfortable and was half-hiding behind Miss Bersager. When Miss Bersager said she was going upstairs, Hazel stood motionless and didn't say anything.

Doris asked, "Miss Bersager is it all right if we move some of the benches and play things into different places?"

"That would be fine, just don't hurt yourselves, or place things too close to the doorway, where the children might get hurt when they're trying to hurry up stairs when the bell rings for dinner."

Doris wanted to make Hazel feel more comfortable, so she invited her to sit with her, near Nancy and Christine, and talk about some plans. Although Hazel didn't express any ideas, she seemed agreeable to everything that was suggested.

Doris took the lead and asked the others to gather the things that the children played with, into one pile on the floor. Happy to have direction, Hazel, Nancy and Christine jumped off their bench and went into action. Things started flying or rolling across the room forming a mound. When one of the girls was accidentally hit by a flying sock doll, there was a muffled giggling. Soon there was out and out laughing, and the occasional, accidental brush turned into a challenge to see who could hit the other one with something soft before they could duck or jump to get out of the way.

Doris was busy moving furniture. The seat portion of the benches lifted up and there was room for storage inside. The benches had been lined up against the walls, but now Doris was moving them around, to create a big playhouse. One area became the kitchen; another space was a living room.

That being done, she worked hard in a different corner. She actually seemed to get so lost there; she didn't realize the other three girls were finished and waiting for more directions.

Finally, Christine said, "O.K, Doris, now what do you want us to do?"

Doris was startled by Christine's question and it brought her attention back to the over-all project.

"Okay," she said, looking around, "great job. Now will you please move all the kitchen things into the kitchen?"

"What kitchen?" they asked.

Doris walked into the *newly constructed kitchen* and showed them that what they were seeing as benches were really stoves, and cabinets, and the one with the basin on it was the sink.

Once the girls saw what was so vivid in Doris's mind, they became almost as excited as she was. They put the pots and pans on one shelf, dishes on another and cups on the edges. With their imaginations sparked, they found all sorts of things to decorate this new kitchen with.

Doris and Hazel decided they should make some of the benches form a classroom. Hazel began to work in that corner of the room. She even found a little chalkboard and a tiny piece of chalk, for her classroom.

With Christine and Nancy still busy in the kitchen, and Hazel's classroom all ready for her students to arrive; Doris invited Hazel to the corner where she had been investing all of her time and attention.

"Hazel, would you help me fold the blankets to make beds in the hospital?"

"Hospital?" Hazel questioned, then seeing how Doris was arranging the blankets, she said, "What a great idea. There was a make-believe "thing" the doctor uses to listen to your chest, over there, would you like me to bring it into the hospital?"

"Thanks, Hazel, that would be great."

The girls were having such a wonderful time "playing" as they were "working," that when Miss Bersager returned to check on them, they suddenly felt guilty. Miss Bersager was delighted! "What a wonderful job you have done. This room has never looked so good! I see a class room and a kitchen and …what is this room?"

"It's a hospital," Doris said proudly. "I'm going to be a nurse."

"That's wonderful, Doris," said Miss Bersager. "There are a few things over there on the floor. Do you think you could put them into one of the benches?"

"Oh sure, Miss Bersager, we just haven't gotten to them, yet."

"Good job, girls. Now if you will just finish wiping off the window sills and the shelves with these cloths, and then sweep the floor, your job will be finished!"

All four of them scurried to move the few remaining things off the floor and put them neatly into the benches. Hazel wiped the windowsills, Nancy and Christine dusted the shelves and Doris swept the floor. Meeting at the doorway, with broom and rags still in their hands, the newly bonded foursome surveyed their accomplishments. They put their arms around each other's shoulders in celebration, as they realized that even more than the exceptional job they had done and the fun they had, they all had made a new friend. And the day wasn't even half over!

Up on the main level, they noticed that there were still girls of all ages scurrying about doing their chores. Some were wiping the furniture, some the windowsills, and some had rags tied onto their feet and were sliding back and forth, dusting and polishing the beautiful wooden steps.

Miss Bersager came and took the rags and broom from the *playroom girls* and told them they were the first to be finished and ready to go up stairs and change the sheet on their beds.

Oh, Doris thought - *Now the new clothes must be on our bed*. She was so hopeful that she ran up those steps faster than she had so far. Hazel was in the room with the next-older girls. She said, "See you later" at the top of the stairs, and went into her room to change her sheet.

Disappointed again, there was only one sheet on their bed; no new clothes. Doris tried to include Christine in pulling the old sheet off and putting the new one on. Mamma had shown Doris how to make what she had called hospital corners, and Doris tried to explain this to Nancy and Christine. They did seem to try, but Doris felt the sheets would be more likely to stay put the whole week, if she tucked them a little more tightly, than the younger girls were able to do.

With the sheets in place, the girls spread their three blankets on the top, and this job was also finished. Doris poked her head into the next room where Hazel had just finished her bed, and asked, "Hazel, what do we do with the sheets we took off the beds?"

Hazel said, "We make a big pile of them at the top of the stairs, then when everyone has put their sheet on the pile, we roll them down the steps and then put them in the cart that one of the boys rolls over from the laundry room."

More of the girls were finishing their chores and the pile of sheets was almost as tall as Christine and Nancy. Soon they would roll it down the clean steps. Still, Doris wondered, *when were the new clothes going to come?* But before the sheet-mountain tumbled or the new clothes appeared on their bed, the bell that called them to lunch rang.

The four play room workers hurried over toward the dining room. Doris picked Alert up, in the playroom, and said, "Oops. Alert and I have to take a trip up to the Tots's room. Go ahead into the dining room," she said to the others. "Alert and I will be in as soon as his diaper is changed."

When she laid Alert in his crib, she noticed a small pile of clothes at the bottom of the crib. She wondered if someone had left his or her play clothes there, by mistake.

When Alert was all cleaned up, she looked through the pile. There was one set of play clothes and a clean pair of pajamas, a pair of socks and one undershirt. *Surely, this isn't what Dottie meant when she said we all get new clothes on Saturday. Or was it?*

Doris kept her thoughts to herself, and brought Alert down to the dining room for lunch. Miss Johnson had already said grace for the food, so Doris held Alert's hands in hers, and said their Norwegian prayer.

Alert happily fed himself the macaroni and cheese by the fists full. Doris enjoyed the food, but lurking in the back of her mind, was that little pile of clean, but wrinkled clothing that was on Alert's bed. She had worn the same blue dress from home, to school all week and she was really looking forward to a new dress. *What if she got an old, wrinkled dress in her pile, and what if she had to give up the pretty dress she had brought from home?*

Lunch was over and the children were officially dismissed. Doris settled Alert in his crib for a nap, and Oscar on his bed for a rest, before going back to her room. Now instead of being excited about that pile of clothes on her bed, she was almost afraid to look. Christine took care of that.

When Doris got to the top of the stairs, Christine was sitting there with a pile of clean, but mostly wrinkled clothes in her lap. Her eyes were red, and the top piece of clothing was wet - with Christine's tears!

"Doris, look!" Christine cried. "This is the pile of clothes that was on our bed! They're not new clothes, these are old clothes, and they're not really ours. I've never seen any of them before!"

Doris didn't know what to say to Christine. They went back to their room and spread the clothing on the bed. There were two pair of under pants, two pair of socks that had been darned to fix holes in each of the heels, two night gowns, two dresses for play that had only a hint of color left in them, and two neatly ironed dresses for school and Sundays. They were the ugliest, oldest dresses either Christine or Doris had ever seen.

"Oh Doris, what will we do?" asked Christine.

"I don't know," said Doris, whose heart had sunk inside of her. "Let me think about it." Doris went down to her thinking spot on the steps. There were children coming and going through the entry room, but she continued to struggle with her thoughts.

Christine calmed down a bit, upstairs. Nancy wasn't in the room, yet, so carefully, without messing the neat little pile, Christine looked through Nancy's clothes. The dress for school was a different color, but all the other things were pretty much the same. While she waited for Doris to return, Nancy came in. For the first time, Christine noticed that the play clothes that Nancy had been wearing since she met her, were just like the ones she had in her "new" pile. Come to think of it, Nancy's school dress was a lot like the *new* ones she and Doris had on their bed.

Christine hadn't noticed that the other girls's clothes looked old before, or that they had worn the same thing every day. She looked around the room, and noticed that everyone else had the same kind of play clothes - worn out, faded dresses. Christine wasn't sure whether she should start to cry again, or just accept the clean clothes and go outside or downstairs to play.

She watched as Nancy gathered her pile of clothes and put them in the box under her bed, except for the nightgown, which she tucked between the sheet and her blankets, so it would be ready to put on after her bath tonight.

"Do you want to go down in the playroom?" she asked Christine.

"Yes, do you want to bring our dolls?" Christine answered.

Okay," said Nancy.

Nancy reached under her bed and took her twenty-inch doll with long blond, wavy hair, white socks, black shoes and a silky party dress, out of the box under her bed. Christine reached into the pillowcase under her bed and pulled out her three-inch doll that was naked except for having a red shirt painted on it. Without even a momentary consideration about which doll was fancier or easier to carry, or bigger or better, the girls happily went downstairs to play.

When they passed Doris on the bottom step, Doris was surprised to see Christine looking cheerful. Christine's crisis seemed to have ended. Christine and Nancy looked equally happy to be going back to the playroom, this time to actually play.

Although she wished she was ready to play, Doris had still not come to a resolution. She tried to speed up her thoughts. *I really don't like wearing the same dress to school every day. At home, Christine and I each had two school dresses. Mamma and then Aunt Jessie, washed them every week, and hung them on the line out the window to dry, then ironed them. Neither Mamma nor Aunt Jessie is here to wash my dresses. I don't have a clothesline, or laundry soap. Even if I could wash my own dresses, it wouldn't really be fair to the other girls for me to be the only one who has two school dresses.*

Doris wanted this discussion with herself to be over. The voices of children playing in her newly designed playroom made it hard to concentrate. She put her fingers in her ears and squeezed her eyes closed. She searched her thoughts and feelings, and realized that what she was feeling about having one well-used, but clean and ironed dress to wear to school every day next week, was a lot like she felt when she was first told she would be in the second grade again. Then she remembered how she had quickly and completely planned to trust that the school decision, which she had no part in making, would be taken care of by God. She remembered her conversation with Jesus in the bathroom and how perfectly peaceful she felt, even before she was changed back into the third grade.

Doris made her decision. She would not pretend that she liked wearing the same dress all week, but she would accept it, without questioning or trying to change it. She was going to trust God and be happy. She would not think any more about how she would look or feel in the dress. Doris was eager to go and play, but before she left her thinking step, she first wanted to think about the things she was thankful for. She had a warm bed, a new Home, closeness to her brothers and sister, she was able to be helpful to Miss Flotten, she was making new friends and her new teacher seemed to like her. Before she opened her eyes again, she took her fingers from her ears, folded her hands together and said, "Thank you, God." When she opened her eyes again, she thought, *I wonder if when Dottie told me about the new clothes, she just said clean clothes. Oh well.*

Before going downstairs to the playroom, Doris went upstairs. She found herself singing, "This is the day, this is the day that the Lord has made, I will rejoice, I will rejoice and be glad in it." Reaching under her bed, she pulled her little doll with the red shirt painted on it from the pillowcase, deciding, he would be the first patient in her new hospital.

Chapter 13
Nurse Doris

*L*ater in the afternoon, the Tots were brought over to the playroom. Nurse Doris now had two live patients for her hospital. First she examined Oscar. She had him lay on the hospital bed, which was a blanket on the floor, while she examined him. She carefully listened to his heart, then watched his breathing, and counted his breaths while watching her invisible watch. Then she made believe she took his temperature and checked his eyes and ears. Once she determined he was well enough to leave the hospital, Doris began to examine her next patient.

It was hard to get Alert to lie still, but she continued his examination, as any professional nurse would. When she was looking into his ears, she noticed that he had a red spot behind one of his ears and several more on his neck under his hair. Nurse Doris called Oscar back again, to be sure she hadn't missed this on him, but he had no red spots. Doris had been enjoying playing in her hospital while all the other children were enjoying the other areas and games. She didn't want the play to stop, but now she felt that a real nurse should check her brother's red spots.

Oscar had moved over to play near Christine and Nancy, so Doris decided to take Alert to the brick building and see if Miss Flotten was in her little room in the back.

Her door was closed, so Doris knocked. "Come in," was the response.

"Miss Flotten, I just noticed a red spot behind Alert's ear and more under his hair in the back. Would you look at him?"

Miss Flotten felt Alert's forehead. "He doesn't seem to have a fever. He doesn't appear ill, or even uncomfortable," she said. But "Oh No," were her next words, as she lifted the hair in back of Alert's neck. "Let me get my magnifying glass."

Returning with a large, round magnifying glass and a comb, Miss Flotten raised Alert's curls up off his neck, again. This time her words were certain. "Alert has Pediculosis."

That sounded like a dreadful disease to Doris. She was so upset that her legs began to shake, and she had to sit down. "Miss Flotten, will he have to go to the hospital?"

"Oh Dukken," she answered, "Pediculosis is just the medical name for head lice."

Unfortunately, Doris was familiar with the term head lice. She and Christine had had head lice when they lived in Elizabeth. Their Mamma used to sit for hours, night after night, combing their hair with a special comb, over a piece of white paper. When the lice or their teeny white eggs landed on the paper, she would squash them. They each had to get haircuts, so it would be easier for Mamma to keep their heads clean. Doris was glad she didn't have head lice; just the thought made her head itchy.

Noticing her scratch her head, Miss Flotten asked, "Can I look at your hair with my magnifying glass?"

"Sure," Doris said, certain that she didn't have a problem.

"Oh No!" Miss Flotten said again. "Are you sure you haven't had an itchy head?"

"No, Miss Flotten, only a tiny bit, but not like when we had head lice in Elizabeth."

"Well, I'm sorry to say, you do have it again. We'll have to do a good check tonight when everyone has a bath, to see if or how many others already have it. You share the bed with Christine, don't you?"

"Yes Miss Flotten," Doris glumly replied, realizing that since their heads were together all night, it was almost certain that Christine also had head lice. Then Doris thought about Nancy and Christine playing so closely together.

"All the Tots will have to be checked, too. Maybe you could help me hold Alert, and I'll give him a haircut right now, then we'll give him a bath by himself, wash his hair, then use the comb like your Mamma used, to get out any lice or nits that are still in his hair."

Doris agreed, though she felt like everything that was making her so happy was now going so wrong. Miss Flotten was able to see the sadness that came over Doris, and she tried to re-assure her. "Doris, you must realize that in a house with as many children as we have, then add all the children each of them come in contact with at school, and I think you will understand that this kind of problem is very usual. Not pleasant for sure, but usual. I always like to think of things like this as a time to grow. It takes patience and persistence to clear this up, and when we have to work real hard at something, it makes us grow up more. We have had, and will have again, many other medical problems that have been worse than head lice. All of our laundry is washed in very hot water, so any lice or nits on the bedclothes or clothing will be killed in the wash. After you and I wash Alert's hair with special shampoo, we will give him clean clothes, a clean sheet and clean blankets. We'll check him carefully each day, and he should be cleared of head lice in about a week. With girls, who have more hair and are together more than boys, it usually takes a little longer, but we will take care of it."

"Unfortunately," she continued, "I am certain that as long as there are children here, we will have to check and treat them for head lice, many times! I will speak with Miss Bersager and Miss Johnson and they will check all the other children. The girls who have lived here long enough, are used to being checked for head lice, and Miss Bersager will not let on if she finds lice in anyone's head, until she can talk to them in private. We'll get you and Christine into the tub by yourselves. You have such beautiful, long hair, Doris. Would you mind having it cut at least a little shorter?"

Doris's hair was so curly that unless she could tie it together, it would fly off in every different direction. She wanted to say *no, I need my hair long*, but instead, she found herself saying, "If it needs to be cut to get rid of the lice, then that would be all right. I can always have it grow long again after the lice are gone."

Miss Flotten and Doris spent the rest of the afternoon together. First taking care of Alert, then Miss Flotten shortened Doris's hair, leaving just enough length for it to be gathered together with an elastic band. They talked about a lot of different things. When Doris told Miss Flotten, that she already knew how to knit and darn, Miss Flotten invited Doris to come and learn how to sew on the sewing machine she had in her room. Doris loved that idea. Miss Flotten said that she had some scrap materials she thought Doris could use to make some clothes for her doll.

Miss Flotten also said one very special thing to Doris before she went downstairs for dinner. She said, "Doris, you were a very good nurse today. You discovered the red spots on Alert and you brought him to me, so we could start his treatment. If you hadn't done what you did, this could have spread to many more children. Thank you. I'll put the boys to bed tonight so you can go back to your building right after dinner and get your bath early."

Doris thought about what Miss Flotten said, about difficult times are times to grow up. *If that is true,* she thought *this is definitely a time to grow up.* First, the disappointment of the "new" clothes that weren't new, then, finding out that both she and Alert definitely had head lice, and most likely so did Christine and Nancy, and who knows how many others. At least now they would all be working to keep anyone else from getting head lice.

It was dinnertime. The smell of chicken and corn bread and cooked carrots filled the house as soon as the big boys brought the heavy pots over from the kitchen in the big stone house. Doris had Alert walked down the steps with her holding his hand, so he wasn't close to her hair, and she was careful not to get her head close to anyone else while they ate their dinner.

When they were dismissed, Doris calmly settled Alert and Oscar in the playroom and she caught up with Christine and Nancy as they were walking back to the stone building. Doris motioned to Christine that she wanted her to come closer to her, so she could talk privately to her. She quietly explained what she and Miss Flotten found out this afternoon, and that she and Christine would begin to have the same treatment their mother did for them when they lived together in Elizabeth, and they had head lice. Christine didn't seem to remember that, and it sounded very bad, but with Doris's encouragement, she accepted what Doris told her would happen. She returned to Nancy, but didn't tell her what Doris said. They were becoming closer friends, and Nancy was only comfortable when she was with Doris and Christine.

Miss Flotten had spoken to Miss Bersager while the children were eating dinner. When they were finished eating, Miss Bersager had already changed the bedding on Doris and Christine's bed, before anyone else saw her do it. Now she had her magnifying glass ready, and the water was in the tub for the first baths.

Since Nancy had only been at The Home a short time, Miss Bersager explained to her that sometimes it was necessary for all of the Home Kids to have their heads checked for little bugs, called lice that liked to live in people's hair. Miss Bersager didn't see any on Nancy. "Nancy," Miss Bersager said, "tonight just Doris and Christine will get the first bath. Please go wait on your bed, and you can have the next bath, with Agnes and Betty."

Once Nancy had reluctantly left the bathroom, Miss Bersager checked Christine, and as expected, she also had head lice.

After Christine and Doris had their bath, and their hair washed with a special shampoo, Miss Bersager washed out the tub with very hot water, and then she brought them to a little room down stairs. Christine's hair was already short, so she just needed it to be carefully combed. The girls combed each other's hair over a piece of white paper, just as Mamma had done so many times before. Doris was proud of how grown up Christine behaved, and what a good job she did with the comb.

Doris pulled her hair back and fastened it to try to control the curls. Christine's hair was thinner and dried almost right away.

All of the girls from their room had been checked for lice, and then bathed, two at a time, and except for the Hauklands, the water was changed after every other set of bathers. Before they came back upstairs, Miss Bersager told Doris and Christine, "No one else has head lice, so it should be easy to get this problem cleared up pretty quickly. I'll help you comb your hair again tomorrow morning after breakfast, then again in the evening. Get a good night sleep, and don't worry!"

When they got back up stairs, Nancy was sitting on her bed with her hair, soaking wet. She looked like she had been crying. Nancy said, "Next week, can I please take my bath with you two?" The Haukland girls were glad that Nancy was so comfortable with them, but they couldn't make that promise. All they could say, for reasons they didn't want to explain, was, "We'll ask Miss Bersager next week, if that would be all right."

Once they finally lay down, Christine and Doris quickly fell asleep.

Chapter 14
Together Alone

*H*ead lice or not, Sunday or not, it was morning. This was confirmed when Doris rolled over and looked out the window to see the sun shining between the tall buildings in New York City. The overwhelming feeling of joy that lifted her out of bed every morning since she came to The Home and allowed her to be the first one to greet her baby brother each morning, was definitely missing. This morning, although her head wasn't itchy, the memory of yesterday's revelation that she and her sister and baby brother had head lice, felt like a tight, heavy blanket that keep her from getting out of bed.

Every other morning, she would have already walked across the cold wooden floor and onto the even colder tile in the bathroom, where she would be getting dressed in her play clothes, shoes and socks, then putting on her coat, to win the fight against the cold morning she met on her way to the big brick building. This morning she would first have to fight a different foe. Like her battle over the clothes, and being put back into the second grade, this was another one that had to do with feelings.

She reached up to touch her soft, curly hair. Several inches had been cut off and carefully thrown away to keep the lice from spreading. She really liked having long hair. She could hear herself saying *it will grow back again*, but right now, it was gone, and she couldn't help feeling sad.

Although Miss Bersager and Miss Flotten were being kind and careful not to tell the others that Doris, Christine and Alert were the ones who triggered the head lice examinations, Doris knew that soon, at least the older children would figure that out. She and Christine would have to bring notes to school on Monday, and what about Sunday School today? How long would it take to get rid of the head lice and feel normal again - whatever normal was, now?

Because of the bugs, everything they had, had to be washed in very hot water. The clothing and even the pillow cases Aunt Jessie gave them to use as suitcases, had to be put into a hot laundry and would be mixed in with all of the other children's things. They had nothing but their little dolls, and memories from their lives in Elizabeth.

It seemed like the will to get out of bed this morning wasn't quiet strong enough to beat the sadness that kept Doris under the covers. The only thing that had made her feel better, when she felt that way after her mother died, was crying. The tears were already in her eyes. She didn't want to cry, especially not here in front of anyone who might be awake or who would wake up if she accidentally made a noise.

Holding her head tipped slightly back and her eyes wide open so the tears wouldn't spill out, Doris carefully slipped from under the covers. Her clothes weren't hard to gather - there were no choices to make, so she bundled them together and went to the bathroom. There was no line, but she could see older girls beginning to get up, as she passed their room. The bathroom would not be the place to cry. She used the bathroom, then quickly pulled her clothes on, right over her night gown, tucking it into her underpants. Carrying her shoes and socks with her, she went down stairs, but not just one flight, she went all the way down to the empty playroom.

As she was putting the socks over her already cold feet, the tears could no longer be contained. Doris continued dressing until her shoes were on and tied before she began to sob. She now felt comfortable in the hospital corner of the playroom, and she took a blanket from one of her hospital beds and held it over her face, as the tears fell, and the sobs repeatedly squeezed her ribs.

The sobbing eventually stopped, and Doris noticed that the light coming in the playroom window was definitely brighter than when she first came down. She was not sure exactly how much time had passed, but she was quite sure, that her baby brother, with his handsome, new haircut would be waiting for her. With one last wipe across her cheeks, just to be sure she hadn't missed any tears Doris left the playroom. There was no decision made, no resolution formulated, but for whatever reason, she now felt ready to face the new day. This was the first full Sunday of their new life together.

Alert looked older with his big-boy haircut. His toothy smile helped Doris feel better, and when she pulled him out of his crib and held him against her chest, so their heads weren't together, she felt comforted. Although happiness wasn't truly there yet, she was able to remember how happy she had been feeling before the head lice, and believe that soon this embarrassing, bothersome problem would be gone and her feelings of joy could come back.

In just a moment, Alert began to wiggle, indicating he was ready to get going. Doris managed to channel his attention to a toy as he lay down for a good spot washing and diaper change. Soon, he was all dressed and ready to play with the toy, in his crib, until some of the other Tots were up.

As she looked around to see what else she could do, Miss Flotten came from the back of the large room. Many of the little ones were still asleep. So without a sound, Miss Flotten waved her hand, to call Doris back to speak to her.

They stepped inside Miss Flotten's room, for privacy and to maintain quiet in the Tots's room. "Dukken, last night we checked every one of the Tots - even and especially Oscar, and not a single one of them had any head lice. You did a wonderful thing to stop this from spreading!"

Tears began to well up in Doris again. She fought them with every bit of courage she could muster, and said, "Thank you Miss Flotten. I hope that soon it will feel good to me."

Realizing that Pediculosis was very difficult for young girls to deal with, Miss Flotten continued. "There are two Tots who have low grade fevers. I will be keeping them home from Sunday School to see if they have any other symptoms, or if the fevers get higher. What if you, Christine and Alert spend the morning here in the Tots's room? I will comb each of your hair and that will bring us another step closer to being finished with this problem. Do you and Christine have dolls?"

"Yes, they are little dolls we got from a missionary to Africa who came to our church," Doris answered.

"Good, you can bring your dolls over, and we can pick out some fabrics and decide what to make. Then, on Monday after school, you could do a little sewing."

Miss Flotten never did any sewing on Sundays. She had a saying that *if you sewed on Sunday, after you die, every stitch you sewed would be pulled out of your nose.* Doris wasn't sure what that meant, except that she wouldn't be doing any sewing on Sunday!

The thought of relaxing and playing in the Tots's room and not getting dressed for Sunday School and having to be worried about giving anyone else head lice, was a huge relief.

"Oh, thank you, Miss Flotten," said Doris. "I don't know what Christine will say, but it sounds like a very nice way to spend the morning. If you don't need me to do anything right now, I will run over and talk to Christine and get our dolls."

"That would be fine, Doris."

"Okay, I will hurry."

Christine also liked the thought of planning some clothes for her doll, and having a morning to relax and play. After breakfast all of the children, including Oscar and Nancy, went to Sunday School in the Chapel, which was across the hall from the dining room in the Boys's building.

Christine, Doris and Alert went back upstairs. The two Tots who had the low-grade fevers were still sleeping. Doris had a little homework from school, which she fit in while Christine was having her hair combed. When the sleeping Tots woke up, their fevers were gone. They played quietly by themselves, after Doris helped them get dressed.

The fabrics were brightly colored, since they had never been in the hot water wash, and since their dolls were so small, there was enough fabric for several different outfits. Miss Flotten had two shoeboxes, one for each of the girls to keep their dolls and soon their doll's clothing in.

"Thank you," Doris said, "we used to keep our dolls in pillow cases we got from our Aunt Jessie, but they had to be put in the hot laundry, so now we can keep them in these shoe-boxes."

Miss Flotten showed them how to make a pattern out of old newspaper, by laying their dolls on the paper and tracing around them, then adding a little more room to stitch the pieces together. Next, they cut the pattern out and pinned it to the cloth. Sometimes the cloth was doubled over, and sometimes it was pinned onto a single layer. They cut some of the pieces out and even pinned the edges. Once they were stitched together, maybe tomorrow, they would see what it would look like and make sure it would fit on their dolls. Miss Flotten said Christine was too young to use the machine, but tomorrow after school, Doris would practice stitching some scraps of material with the machine, and then she would be able to sew the things they had cut out, and pinned.

Both Doris and Christine enjoyed this special time very much and Alert was happy and calm having his sisters near him as he played. He was still unhappy when they left him to go to school or to the other building to sleep. He would have to learn, with time, that they were only a short distance away, and that despite the little separations, this was the new home for all of the Haukland children.

Miss Flotten noticed how peaceful Alert looked as he was playing by their feet and said, "Alert must have missed you, the weeks he was here without you. He looks so content now."

"What do you mean, Miss Flotten?" asked Doris.

"Alert and Oscar came here a few weeks before you and Christine, didn't they?"

"Oh yes, but they weren't with us before they came here. Oscar and Alert were at our Tante Ulla's house for about a year before they came here."

"I didn't know that," Miss Flotten said. "Then your mother didn't die recently?"

"No, our mother went into the hospital just after Christmas, last year. That's when the boys went to stay with Tante Ulla. Everyone hoped that soon our Mamma would come home, but she didn't. After she died, the boys stayed with Tante Ulla until they came here, to this Home. Alert was only a year and a half and Oscar turned four just after our Mamma died."

"Oh, Dukken, no wonder you are all so happy to be together again."

Perhaps Pappa was the only one who could really understand the loss and confusion both Oscar and Alert must have felt when their mother, sisters, and father disappeared from their lives. They were suddenly in a new house with a new family except for each other. Then just a few weeks ago they lost the new family they had when they came to the Home; a father, mother and sister named Alice, who was eleven years old.

It was hard enough for Doris and Christine to understand what happened to their mother, but at least they saw their father more often and they knew their mother didn't *want* to leave them. She got sick and couldn't get better. So she died and went to live in Heaven with Jesus. Oscar and Alert were too young to understand these very difficult words. All they knew was that people they loved and trusted suddenly were gone - twice!

After lunch they all went back upstairs. When Oscar came up to the Tots's room to change his clothes after Sunday School, he was a little crabby. He seemed to feel he had missed out on some fun.

With a little less self-consciousness about her head lice, after a good combing, with very few nits (the eggs that would hatch into lice if they weren't removed from the hair) and no lice found, Doris helped Oscar out of his Sunday clothes and into his play clothes. She teased him, keeping the shirt over his head, with his arms still stuck in the sleeves, so he couldn't see anything. Then she'd scoot away from him and call, "come find me." She was careful that he didn't run into anything that might hurt him. Doris enjoyed watching Oscar's mood change from gloomy into happy. Doris continued to devote extra attention to this very pleasant, almost five year old boy, for the rest of the day.

When Oscar was playing with Christine and Alert, Miss Flotten asked Doris: "Did the boys know their Tante Ulla well when they went to stay with her?"

"No. Our Mamma went to work every day. She was a nurse. In the morning we'd all leave together. Mamma brought Christine to kindergarten, and I brought the boys to a nursery, then she went to work and I went to first grade. Tante Ulla lived in Elizabeth, too, but her house was too far for us to walk to. Besides, Mamma didn't have any time to visit. On days we didn't have school or work, we did laundry and cleaned, and in the evenings, we were busy cooking, sewing or knitting, giving babies baths and everything else."

"Now I know where you learned to be so helpful, Dukken."

Doris smiled. Although she hadn't wanted to think or talk about Mamma, because it usually made her cry, this time she didn't feel like crying and she noticed that for some reason it felt good to tell Miss Flotten about their life before and since Mamma died.

Miss Flotten said, "I know all of the children who come here, have been through difficulties. That's why they're here, and it takes them time to adjust. But I wish I had known what these young boys had gone through when they first arrived here.

"We're not used to having children younger than three years old. Alert is the youngest child in The Home right now. He is the only one still in diapers. When he first got here, we tried to make him go on his knees to say the nighttime prayer, and do some of the other things the others do, but he fussed and wouldn't do it. We hollered at him because we thought he was being rebellious. I guess he was just being what he is - too young to understand."

After Doris and Miss Flotten talked about the way things were before they came to The Home, Doris noticed that she felt the same kind of comfort she got when she cried, only without the tears and the sore ribs. Talking about what had happened before they came to the home seemed to help Doris move those things into the back of her thoughts, and make room for new ones.

Before they went down for dinner, Doris wanted Miss Flotten, to know about *her promise*. "Miss Flotten, before my mother died, she asked me to keep our family together. We can't have Pappa here, except to visit every other Sunday, but now all four of us children are together, and it feels so good. Now, Christine and I are even beginning to feel like our family is growing each time we make a new friend.

"Today started out as a sad day for me. I hate that we have Pe-dil-i-co-sis, or however you say that word, and I would still like it if we were all back in Elizabeth with our mother, but being up here with my brothers and sister today made me feel a lot better. I feel like my sadness is over and tomorrow I will be happy again."

Miss Flotten said "I had a special day, too. I'll see you in the morning, Dukken, and after school we can practice sewing."

"Thanks, Miss Flotten, I can't wait."

Chapter 16

Oscar's Birthday Party With Pappa

*M*onday morning, even though she and Christine would carry notes to school, telling the teachers they had head lice, Doris was still looking forward to starting her second week of school in Fort Lee. As soon as her eyes opened and saw a hint of morning, she was up, dressed and reporting for the job, with her brothers and the rest of the Tots. Miss Flotten told her several times, she didn't have to come over so early, but she also told her how much Doris was helping her by being there to get the day started on a good note.

School went well. Doris knew the teacher received the letter from the nurse, but neither she nor the teacher said anything about that to each other. Doris longed to blend in with the class. None of the students knew they all had to be checked for head lice by the school nurse and bring a note home to their mothers to watch for this, because of someone in their class. They even sent a note home with Doris and checked her as they did all the other children, so she wouldn't seem any different. Doris secretly jumped for joy inside, but outside she acted perfectly calm, when the school nurse didn't find any lice or nits in her hair.

When she got home, she ran right to the Tots's room, calling, "Miss Flotten, Miss Flotten - guess what!"

Miss Flotten hurried out of her room, concerned that something was wrong, but when she saw Doris, she knew it was good news.

"The school nurse found No Nits and No Lice!"

Doris jumped in circles clapping her hands and singing, "No Nits and No Lice!"

Miss Flotten smiled, then she said, "I have the sewing machine all set up for you, are you ready to do some sewing?"

Christine and Nancy were playing with Alert and Oscar, so Doris calmed herself enough to sit down, and Miss Flotten began teaching her what to do. The machine had what was called a treadle near the floor that Doris had to keep pumping. She had to stretch a little to reach it, but before long, she was able to keep it moving at a nice steady pace. Miss Flotten had her practice starting and stopping the treadle, which seemed to be even harder than keeping it moving. When the treadle moved, it made the needle go up and down. Once she mastered controlling the treadle, she was ready to thread the needle and learn how to direct the fabric she was sewing, so the needle would go through the fabric where she wanted it to be. At first, it was hard to put everything together, but to everyone's delight, Doris caught on quickly and was able to use her hands to hold and move the material and her feet to keep the machine running. After about an hour of practice, she was able to sew one outfit for Christine's doll, and one for her own.

Each day after school, Doris did a little more sewing. She also found time to play with her brothers, help out with the Tots in the morning and evening, and still do a very good job with her homework.

Rooted

By Sunday morning, it had been a whole week with no lice or nits in anyone's hair. What relief they all felt! She loved the early morning greeting from Alert, and feeling free to hug and snuggle him without concerns of head lice. This made their time together even more wonderful.

This Sunday was extra special for two reasons. "Miss Flotten," Doris said when she saw her in the Tots's room, "this is the day our Pappa will come to visit us, *and* we will have a little birthday party for Oscar!"

"That will be nice, Doris. When is Oscar's birthday?"

"I just remember it is in January. Hazel told me that there is only one birthday party a year, for everyone, so we decided not to make a fuss over it. Pappa's visit will be like a little party for just our family."

"I wonder if your father will recognize Alert with his new hair cut?" Miss Flotten responded. Then she seemed distracted in thought. "Doris, a few brand new sailor suits came in last week. I wonder if any of them would fit Oscar and Alert. Would you like to try them?"

"That would be fun!" Doris responded. Miss Flotten brought three hangers with outfits that someone had donated. Each outfit was a different size. First, Miss Flotten handed Doris the smallest suit. "Do you think this will fit Alert?"

Doris had washed him and given him a new diaper. "This is like playing Dolls, Miss Flotten," Doris said as she slipped the shirt over Alert's head. It fit him perfectly, so she put the pants on, too. "Alert!" said Doris, "you look so handsome!"

The encouragement delighted Alert whom until that time hadn't been as fond of the activity as Doris was. She brought him into Miss Flotten's room where there was an oval mirror over her dresser. "See, Alert" said Doris pointing to the mirror, "see how handsome you look?

Today Pappa will come to visit us, and you can wear this new suit when he comes."

Doris never knew exactly what Alert understood, but he seemed happy with the over-all conversation, and he especially enjoyed looking at himself in the mirror. "Do you think he could wear this to Sunday School, too?"

"I guess that would be all right, Dukken," said Miss Flotten, "but let's take it off until after breakfast. It smells like pancakes, and you know how messy that will be."

Alert refused to lift his arms to slip them out of the sleeves, making Doris firmly but gently pull his arms through one at a time, while he pulled away from her. Either he didn't like the idea of taking the suit off because he liked it, or he was finished playing dolls and didn't want his clothes changed any more. But he only fussed until he was fully dressed in his play clothes and ready for breakfast.

Oscar was next. He had barely gotten back from the bathroom when Doris said "Look, Oscar. Miss Flotten gave us this new suit to wear when Pappa comes to visit us today!" Oscar eyed the suit with a lot less enthusiasm than Doris showed, but he agreed to try it on.

"Miss Flotten," Doris called, "can we try on the bigger suit. This one is kind of tight."

Miss Flotten brought the next size, which fit perfectly. Unlike Alert, Oscar was very glad to have the suit taken off, and to be allowed to put his play clothes on, and get down to those pancakes he woke up smelling.

Again, Doris helped out with the other Tots as they dressed for breakfast, and she promised Miss Flotten that she'd come back upstairs after breakfast, to get their sticky hands and faces washed, and help them get dressed for Sunday School. Since the Tots don't go to school, they had special clothes to wear just for Sunday School. Some of the

Tots needed a lot of help, but the older ones only needed help tying their shoes and making sure their clothes weren't on backwards.

Before breakfast, Miss Johnson (the older boys nurse) said: "I would like to read two verses from Proverbs, chapter eight.

Verse 32: "Now therefore hearken unto me, O ye children: for blessed are they that keep my ways. And verse 33. Hear instruction, and be wise, and refuse it not."

"Let us pray. Today is Sunday, Lord, we look forward to worshiping you, and hearing even more of your word. Please open our ears to hear and help us remember and obey your word. Please bless this food to our bodies, and us to your service. In Jesus name, Amen."

After the blessing, the children were eager to start eating what they had been looking forward to, since they first woke up to the wonderful aromas. Doris cut Alert's pancakes with her fork, and made a little syrup puddle in the middle of his plate. Holding his fork in his fist, Alert stabbed one piece at a time, dipped it in the little puddle, then with drops of syrup forming a trail from the plate up the towel that covered his shirt and into his mouth, he carefully inserted the little fork into his mouth. With every bite, he smiled broadly and said "mmm" as he chewed.

Oscar, Christine and Nancy all enjoyed the pancakes, too. By now, they all knew that when they wanted something that wasn't on their table, they raised their hand, and one of the bigger girls brought it to them.

They all had fun trying to use the dining room sign language. Oscar had learned to make the M, B and S, and he practiced by pointing to something on the table and making the sign for the first letter. They were all pretty slow in making each letter, and it often wound up with all of them laughing, having no idea what the other one was saying, but they kept trying, so they could be more like the other kids.

The line was long for the Tots to get their hands and faces washed. Doris and Miss Flotten worked as quickly as they could. Once each of the Tots could touch things without having them stick to their fingers, they were ready to get their Sunday clothes on. With all the Tots dressed and ready, Doris ran back to the girls's building and changed her own clothes.

This was the first day she would wear her 'new' school and Sunday dress this week. Yesterday, she had gotten a pretty green dress, with a sash that tied in the back. The dress had been carefully ironed, and Doris had laid it out so it wouldn't get wrinkled. Mostly, she tried hard not to pay any attention to her clothing, except to make sure it was on right and all the buttons were buttoned and the sash was tied in a neat bow.

Some of the older children walked into town on Sunday evenings to go to the Mission for church, but the younger children met in the Chapel that was opposite the dining room. Last week, Doris had passed the Chapel when it was all set-up for Sunday School, but she hadn't really looked in. The room had long benches on each side, and a long narrow rug ran down the aisle between the seats. In the front, there was a big beautiful picture of a shepherd with his sheep, and there were large windows without individual panes on both sides of the room. Doris was surprised that a room that really looked and felt like a little church was always behind the two doors opposite the dining room that she never even noticed until last week.

Miss Bersager played the piano, and all the children sang along. Then Mr. Ortlip, an artist, drew a picture with chalk on a large piece of paper held up on a three-legged stand, while he told a Bible Story. This morning it was about a crowd of over five thousand people who were hungry, but they were far out in the country where they couldn't buy bread. There was a boy with five small barley loaves and two small fish. Jesus had the people sit down on the grass, and he performed a miracle. He took the loaves and said a prayer to give thanks and then gave everyone who was sitting some bread. He did the same thing with the fish. Everyone had as much as they wanted to eat and there were twelve baskets left over. Jesus was careful not to waste any. The picture was very pretty and Mr. Ortlip left it so the children could look at it during the week.

After Sunday School, the Tots headed back up stairs to change into their play clothes, before dinner. Oscar agreed to keep the sailor suit on until Pappa left, but he made Doris promise that he would only have to get dressed up today, for the first visit with all four of them. Oscar said, "The other boys will laugh at me and I won't be able to play, wearing this suit."

The Hauklands weren't used to this, but on Sunday, lunch was called *dinner,* and it was the kind of food they had for *supper* on school days. Then in the evening, they had *lunch* food for *supper*.

Father Nelson said grace, at *dinner,* and everyone ate a very special meal of ground beef, mashed potatoes with gravy, peas, carrots, and applesauce. Oscar held up his hand, his thumb and pinky together and three middle fingers pointing down, making an "M" and Doris poured him a glass of milk, almost without thinking of what a big accomplishment this was.

An oatmeal cookie ended the delicious meal, and Doris quickly wiped Alert's face, and directed Christine and Oscar to wipe off their milk mustaches, before Father Nelson came in and dismissed them. This time, although they weren't one of the first, they did join the crowd of children bursting out of the dining room. Most of the children were going to the stone building to play for the afternoon, but the Hauklands were going to meet or wait for Pappa, in the entry room.

When they got up the three wide steps in the hallway, there was Pappa - standing in the middle of the room, waiting for them! Pappa had gotten there before they did and he had already taken care of the business of putting the check to pay for their care, into a box just inside Father Nelson's office and had caught his breath, which took several minutes, after walking up that steep hill.

Doris thought, Pappa's visit is the most wonderful thing that happened since they were all together on Easter at Tante Ulla's house. The room mostly had single chairs, so they pulled a few of them close together, to make a little circle. At that moment, none of them noticed the brown paper bag on the seat next to Father Nelson's doors, they just wanted to celebrate being with Pappa.

The children were so small that two of them easily fit on one chair. Doris and Christine both started to talk at once. They had each saved their best stories to tell Pappa. Pappa smiled and said, "Wait, I wish I could hear you all at once, but I can only listen to one of you at a time. First I want to say Happy Birthday, Oscar. You are five years old! I am so proud of you, son."

"Thank you, Pappa. I feel very grown up now."

Pappa shook Oscar's hand, then hugged him, but without taking him onto his lap, as he might have, if Oscar was only four. Pappa asked Oscar, "Did you get to play outside in the snow?"

Oscar said, "A little, but I still didn't slide down the steep hill.

Pappa said, "Maybe next year you will be more comfortable to try that. It is indeed a very steep hill, so I'm glad you will wait until you feel ready."

Then Pappa looked at Alert, and said, "Have you learned any new words?"

Alert beamed, realizing he was the center of attention. He seemed to have understood what Pappa asked, but he didn't even try to say anything. Instead, he proudly forced the middle three fingers of his right hand to stand up using his left hand to hold the thumb and little finger and help him spread his middle fingers slightly apart. At first no one knew what he was doing, but suddenly Christine said, "I know - he's saying water," she said. All the children laughed as Christine explained the mealtime language, and that Alert was making a "W" for water. Oscar then demonstrated the letters he learned to ask for milk, sugar and butter.

Pappa got a good laugh at Alert's silent word, then he looked at Christine, and asked, "How are you doing, Christine."

Christine said, "Pappa I have a wonderful new friend. Her name is Nancy." Christine wanted to run right upstairs to see if she could find Nancy, so Pappa could meet her, but he said, "Maybe next time I come I'll have time to meet Nancy."

"And Doris?" said Pappa. "Father Nelson tells me that you are not only helping your brothers and sister, but many of the other children here, as well. He said that since you and Christine came to be with your brothers, that so much good has happened. Do you feel happy here? Are you working too hard?"

Doris wanted to say so many things to Pappa. There must have been a hundred times these past two weeks that she said to herself, *I can't wait to tell Pappa about this,* but now she didn't know where to begin!

"Pappa, I am very happy here. Every morning I go to the Tots's room and help Miss Flotten until it's time for breakfast. Miss Flotten is teaching me to sew on a sewing machine, and I have made some clothes for my doll and for Christine's doll."

She barely took a breath before she continued. "Saturday morning we all have jobs to keep the big houses clean, and Christine and I got to clean up the playroom. We had so much fun doing it, that it didn't even feel like we were working."

Doris could have gone on and on, but when she paused to think of the next thing, she noticed that Pappa looked very tired. Instead of continuing to tell him all about school and her make-believe hospital, and every other part of her new life, she asked, "Pappa, do you like living with Tante Ulla's sister-in-law, in Brooklyn?"

Pappa hesitated a little before he answered. "Its fine, Doris. It is much better than living all alone in our old house and instead of four hours to get here; it only took me two hours. Mrs. Boardsen is very kind, and she cooks meals for me every day."

Doris thought Pappa didn't look like he was eating a lot. He looked very thin, and he had to stop talking and cough a few times. Even though Pappa's words were saying he was glad to be at Mrs. Boardsen's house, Doris thought he still looked very sad. She decided it wouldn't be nice to make Pappa talk any more about his new home.

Pappa had brought a paper bag with some candy and hand made toys for his children. One of Pappa's favorite things to do was to take a piece of wood, and use his knife to make something out of it. Doris had watched him many times, as he sat on the step in front of their house in Elizabeth and little chips of wood piled up around his feet as he carved something.

Pappa reached in the bag and pulled out 4 little wooden toys he had carved. Doris and Christine got a man hanging on a string that was tied to the top of each of two six-inch long sticks. When they held the bottom of the sticks and pulled the sticks apart, the man swung around and around, doing acrobatic tricks on the string. Alert laughed when he watched them playing with it, but Pappa said it would be dangerous for Alert because he might get poked in the eye with the long, thin sticks.

Alert got a little carved tugboat, and Oscar got a figure of a boy with a hockey stick. Pappa said, "Next time I come, I'll bring you another one, so you can play the game with some one else." Oscar liked that thought, but he had already gotten off the chair and was making believe the figure was playing hockey on the rug.

Doris said, "Alert, next time you take a bath, you can bring your tugboat in the tub with you." Alert smiled, then he too got down on the floor. Right now, the maroon rug was water to Alert and his tugboat was skidding along like they had seen the ferry boats do, when they lived in Elizabeth.

Five-year-old Oscar said, "Thank you, Pappa. On the side of the brick building, there is a skating rink. Since it has been so cold, it is filled with ice, and the bigger boys use old brooms and an empty can to play hockey. I love to watch them. Once, they let me try it, while they were taking a rest. It was fun. When I get bigger, I want to play with them."

With Oscar's example, Doris and Christine also said, "Thank you, Pappa," and Alert said, "Ta-Ta."

Christine told Pappa, "On Saturdays, we get a pile of very old clothes that we have to wear every single day. The same dress, every day to school," she repeated. All the kids who aren't from the home get to wear a different dress every day."

Doris tried to end that conversation by saying, "It's okay. The clothes have to be washed in hot water every week, so they don't stay very nice. Once we're back at The Home, everyone is dressed kind of the same, so it doesn't matter. The teachers in school understand, and they don't say anything that makes us feel bad. Pappa, can I show you the doll clothes I made?"

"Sure," said Pappa, "can you bring them here?"

"Yes," said Doris - "and Pappa, watch how fast I can go up and down these big steps!"   With that, she ran as fast as she could up the steps, without holding the rail. When she reached the landing, she turned around to make sure Pappa had been watching. His smile and wave let her know he was impressed by her demonstration. With the joy of his approval, Doris continued up the rest of the steps, which were out of Pappa's sight, and she pulled her shoebox out from under the bed.

Back on the landing Doris called; "Are you watching, Pappa?" Then she started down the steps, without holding anything but her shoebox.

"Boy, Doris, you sure are fast and sure on those steps!"

"Look, Pappa, this blue shirt is the first thing I ever made on the sewing machine. It's a little hard to work the machine because I have to reach the pedals and with my feet resting on a big iron mesh treadle, I have to rock my feet back and forth, while I use my hands to place the cloth where it can be grabbed by little teeth under the table, and then the needle goes up and down and makes the stitches. I love doing it. Now look at this yellow shirt. This is the last one I made. See how much straighter the stitches are on this shirt? Miss Flotten says I am a very quick learner. My box is already half full of clothes for my doll, and I have made several shirts for Christine's doll, too."

As they visited, many children came and went through the entry room, and there was another family of children gathered around an older man and woman. Although she had no grandparents to compare them to, Doris decided that this couple must be the children's grandparents. They were all dressed in fancy Sunday clothes. The man wore a grey felt hat and the woman wore a fancy black velvet hat with a black net that mostly covered her hair in the front. They went into the room with the piano, where they were talking together.

Hours passed with the children no longer needing to be directed to allow each other to finish their turn with Pappa's full attention. None of them mentioned the head lice, and except for Christine's tale of the Saturday clothes pile, there was nothing but happiness coming from his children. The change in all four of them since he had left them just two weeks ago was more than he had hoped for, or imagined could be.

As he sat, surrounded by his precious children, he thought, *the memory of each of their beaming faces, and the chatter in my ears will help me through the next two weeks, until I see them again.*

It was starting to get dark outside, and Pappa was working up the courage to tell his children that he had to start back to Brooklyn. Just then Father Nelson came in the front door. He removed his grey felt hat and held it in his left hand. "Magnus," he said, reaching out his right hand. "It's so good to see you. How are you?"

Magnus's answer was given out of courtesy more than honesty. "I'm fine, thank you, Father Nelson, how are you?"

"Very well, thank you," said Father Nelson, then he asked: "Magnus, will you be joining us for supper, tonight?"

"Oh, no thank you," answered Magnus, again out of courtesy, trying to ignore the emptiness in his stomach.

"Oh PLEASE, Pappa," begged Doris. There is so much more we want to tell you, and if you come to supper, you can see what a big boy Alert is when he eats, and you can see how fast the other children are when they use the sign language to talk to each other during the meals."

"And you can meet Nancy, Pappa. Please?"

"Why don't I have the girls in the dining room set an extra place in the staff dining room and you can sit where you'll be able to see your children. Then you can make your trip home with something warm in your stomach?" said Father Nelson.

"Please, please Pappa," added Christine and Oscar, together. With that, Pappa gave in.

"Thank you, Father Nelson, I would be very grateful for the meal and the chance to see more of the wonderful things my children have been telling me, about their days here."

The dinner bell still hadn't rung, but the Hauklands almost propelled Pappa forward as they all held hands and walked over to the brick building. Doris wanted to see if Miss Flotten was there, so Pappa could meet her and she could show Pappa the sewing machine. She also wanted to show Pappa how neatly she had made all the cribs and little beds in the Tots's room, before she left for Sunday School this morning.

"Miss Flotten, Miss Flotten" Doris called, as she saw her in the back of the Tots's room. "Our Pappa is here! May I please show him the sewing machine?"

"Oh, certainly, Dukken," she replied, then seeing the tall thin man with the three other children, she held out her hand and said, "I'm Miss Flotten, and you MUST be Pappa Haukland."

"I do have that honor, Miss Flotten. It is a pleasure to meet you; I have been hearing your name all afternoon. I'm glad for the chance to thank you for all you are doing for my children."

"I don't know what I ever did before Doris came. She is more helpful than three older girls, and I'm sure you can see the big change in the boys - especially Alert. Oscar has always been very cooperative and pleasant. Doris has helped me understand Alert a lot better than I had, and her kindness to him and all the other Tots, is a real gift."

"That's very nice to hear, Miss Flotten," said Pappa.

Machinery always interested Pappa. He inspected every part of the sewing machine, the belts, and wheels, the bobbin on the bottom and the thread on the top.

"But Doris, how do you reach that treadle?" Pappa asked.

"I'll show you, Pappa," Doris said, as she sat on the rickety wooden chair in front of the machine. There was nothing that she wanted more than to show Pappa how she could sew. Miss Flotten brought her a piece of scrap cloth, and she folded it over and stitched the two sides together. "See," she said proudly when she pulled it out from the needle and snipped the threads to free it from the machine.

Pappa was indeed, very impressed with Doris's accomplishment.

The dinner bell signaled them back down stairs, but before they left Miss Flotten's room, Pappa thanked her again, and wished her a good evening.

The children showed Pappa where the staff ate, and he waited at the door for Father Nelson to direct him to the right seat. As he was waiting, Christine jumped out of her seat calling, "Pappa, Pappa!" She called him with so much enthusiasm that Pappa thought there might be a problem. "Here she is! Here's Nancy!"

Pappa came into the children's dining room and reaching way down, he shook Nancy's hand, saying, "How do you do, Nancy, it's a pleasure to meet you." This made both Nancy and Christine feel very special.

Soon all of the children were seated and quiet. Pappa was standing in the doorway between the two dining rooms. The children had already prepared Pappa for the blessing by Father Nelson and the silence that would follow.

Magnus sat next to Father Nelson, where he could see his own children and many others. He found himself trying to "read" the children's sign language, as he ate. Pappa and the children smiled back and forth at each other during the meal, and Doris waved to Pappa and pointed toward Alert, to be sure he noticed the grown-up way Alert was eating and behaving.

Doris had torn his sandwich into smaller pieces, and he was able to eat the sandwich on his own. He needed a little help to keep his spoon level, when he was eating the tomato soup, but there was no misbehavior. Alert readily opened and closed his mouth around the spoon, and didn't miss a drop.

Although now it was very dark, and there would be fewer trolleys, with the warm meal in his stomach, and the warmth in his heart from such a pleasant afternoon with his children, Magnus was glad he had agreed to stay through dinner.

This time the children walked with their father until he started down the hill. It was hard for them to go inside while their father was still walking away, but it was too cold to stand still, outside. "I'll be back on the Sunday after next," he called to them as he turned and started down the hill.

"Bye Pappa," they all called together.

At the bottom of the hill, Magnus recalled his painful emotions of two weeks ago. It was still very hard to leave this property while his children remained here, but having them together and the pure happiness they expressed with their words and actions lifted Magnus's spirits. Again he found himself saying a prayer. This time it was with less pain and even more hope that he said, "Thank you, God, for this Home, and all the caring people who watch over my children. Thank you that not only are they together, but they are each and all happy here. Please continue to watch over them, and give me health and strength to get back to Brooklyn, and to return in two weeks."

Chapter 17
Quarantined

*B*efore her sense of duty lifted her out of the warm bed, the sweet memory of Sunday afternoon with her brothers and sister, and Pappa all together, brought a feeling of calmness and peace to Doris. All the things she worked so hard at holding in her mind for the past two weeks, so she could tell Pappa, had happily been delivered. Now she was ready for more experiences and to plan which ones and how she would tell Pappa on his next visit.

Doris loved the routines and knowing what she could do to be helpful, but she thought as she lay there, it seemed to be the surprise things, the things that just happened, that made the best stories to remember and tell Pappa. Doris stretched her arms and legs all at once being careful not to wake her sister, then she carried her happy feelings with her little pile of clothes into the bathroom.

"Oh, Dukken," said Miss Flotten, as Doris reached the top step inside the brick building. "Three of the Tots are very sick. I have been up all night with them. They are finally sleeping now, but I am too tired to care for the rest of the children this morning."

This was not what Doris was expecting this morning. First, she assured Miss Flotten: "That's okay. You go to bed and I will watch all the children until Tootsie finishes setting the tables in the dining room, and comes to help with the Tots. Which ones are sick?" she asked.

"Bobby, Freddy and Anna," Miss Flotten answered. "I moved them into the infirmary, next to my room. They started with a slight fever, but instead of getting better, their fevers got higher. I have been putting cool cloths on them to lower their temperatures. They don't feel as hot right now, and they are all sleeping soundly. I asked Mary, who came early to start working in the dining room, to go over to Father Nelson and have him call the doctor, but I don't know when the doctor will come."

"Okay, Miss Flotten, I will start to get everyone up and dressed, and then when Tootsie gets here, we will work together."

"Thank you, Dukken," said Miss Flotten. Doris thought how frail and tired Miss Flotten looked as she walked back to her little room.

The Tots's room was still quiet but Doris couldn't wait to give Alert a great big hug! There he was, standing in the corner of his crib waiting for her with his little homemade pacifier still in his mouth. "Give me that silly thing!" she teased, in a low voice, taking the little plug out of Alert's mouth and dropping it back into his crib. Alert laughed, and reached out both arms to be picked up by Doris.

"Would you like to go to the potty?" She asked.

Alert looked at Doris wide-eyed and shook his head.

Though Doris didn't seem to realize it, "sister" didn't fully describe all of the things that she was to Alert. After he finished on the potty, they went back to his crib. Before she started to get him washed, she wrapped both arms around his little body and twisted him from side to side making the hug even better. "Did you sleep well last night?" she asked Alert. He shook his head up and down, but Doris said, "I can't hear you when you shake your head." She asked again, "Did you sleep well last night?"

"Yes"-answered Alert, proud to have understood what Doris meant, and also to be able to clearly say the word.

Doris again held him closer and said, "You are getting so grown up! Let's get you dressed quickly, because today I have to help with all of the other children."

Doris had him lie down and she quickly got him washed and dressed. "One down," she said to him, as she settled him in his crib with a toy. Doris looked around, and noticed that a few of the other children were waking up. Emma was sitting on the side of her bed, and Doris noted she was wiggling. "Good Morning!" she greeted Emma. "Are you ready to go to the bathroom?"

"Yes!" the little girl answered. Doris took her hand and walked her there.

"Do you need any help in the bathroom?" She asked Emma, who was three.

"No," she answered, "I'm a big girl."

"That's great, Emma, I'll put your clothes on the bed, and you can start to get dressed when you are finished."

"Okay, Miss Doris," she answered.

Miss Doris? Thought Doris, *why is she calling me Miss Doris*? Usually Miss Flotten or one of the older girls took care of the other Tots while Doris took care of Alert and Oscar. Today would be different.

Since the infirmary was right near the bathroom, Doris looked in on the sick Tots before returning to the others. She was glad to see they were still asleep. Even from the doorway, she noticed that their faces looked more pink than usual. She decided that probably had to do with the fever.

Loud, frantic crying drew Doris back into the Tots's room. Thomas, who was still under his covers, was screaming and another child was lying sideways, across Thomas's legs. That child was struggling, but unable to get himself up. His arms were each partially into his shirtsleeves, and they were stuck over his head, which was also stuck in his shirt. From inside the shirt, his muffled voice was calling for help.

Doris helped the boy on top, to get back onto his feet. By now, she realized it was Gustav. She calmed Thomas down enough to determine that he was shocked, but not injured. Gustav's muffled voice tried to explain: "I'm sorry Thomas. I was trying to get my shirt on, and I couldn't get it over my head. I need to hurry to the bathroom, and I didn't remember that your bed was in the way. I can't see through this shirt!"

Doris said, "Gustav, tuck your chin down." With that, she tugged the bottom of his shirt, and his head popped through the snug neckline. She twisted him around, putting him on the right path to the bathroom and watched from behind as Gustav's hands finish their journey through his sleeves, and broke free, ready to work.

All was quiet again; however, this noisy incident sped up the usually gradual pace of the other Tots waking up. It seemed like everyone needed attention at the same time. Doris tended to one tiny crisis after the other until all the children were up and dressed for breakfast. Just then, Tootsie arrived.

"Where's Miss Flotten?" she asked.

"She's sleeping. She was up all night taking care of the Tots who are sick," Doris told her.

"I can't believe you have gotten all these children dressed by yourself! Good job! Do you want me to bring them downstairs for breakfast?" Tootsie asked.

Doris, half wondering why Tootsie was asking her what to do, said, "Sure, if it's time for breakfast."

As the parade of Tots was streaming down the stairs toward the inviting smell of breakfast, a tall man dressed in a dark suit and tie and carrying a small black bag in one hand entered the brick building. Tootsie must have looked the closest to an adult, because the man addressed her.

"I am Doctor Andersen. Can you tell me where I can find the children who are sick?"

Tootsie pointed up the stairs and told him they were in the infirmary, at the back of the large room. Doris volunteered to get Miss Flotten. She knew she would want to be there when the doctor was examining the children.

"Good Morning, Miss Flotten," said Dr. Andersen when they were all together in the infirmary. "I'm so glad you have isolated these children." Miss Flotten returned the Doctor's greetings, and then stood quietly behind him as he examined each of the children from head to toe.

"It looks like Scarlet Fever. We'll have to quarantine The Home until we're certain. If it is, we'll keep all the children until there are no additional cases for a week. The sick children will have to remain isolated for about forty days."

Miss Flotten didn't look shocked or surprised, just very tired. This was not a new experience for her. "Is there anything I can give them or do to make them more comfortable?" she asked.

"No," he said. "As you know, we now believe that Scarlet Fever is caused by streptococcus. This germ is easily passed from one person to the other. In the hospitals, they are finding that careful washing of hands, equipment and laundry are a very big part of keeping the germs from spreading. What you are doing to keep their fevers under control and keeping them isolated is the best we can do now. Hopefully, before long, there will be an inoculation that will cure Scarlet Fever."

Dr. Andersen had been coming to the home for many years, and he knew Miss Flotten very well by now. The doctor continued, "I don't think these three will spike such a high fever again. It will be the others you'll have to watch for now. These three all look exactly the same. I'll take a swab from one of them, to culture and then we'll know for sure."

Miss Flotten knew what that meant, so she sat on Bobby's bed to hold his head still and try to comfort him as the doctor put the cotton tipped stick in his mouth and rubbed it against his very sore throat.

"There," said Dr. Andersen. "I'll call Father Nelson as soon as I get the results. Until then, I hope you can get some sleep. You're going to need it, Miss Flotten."

"Thank you Dr. Andersen. Father Nelson will be downstairs eating breakfast. Would you please tell him that we are quarantined?"

"Certainly," he replied as he packaged his specimen and closed his little black bag.

Father Nelson came back into the dining room after breakfast. The children were all positioned to push back their chairs and charge for the door, as soon as he said 'You're dismissed,' however, after speaking with Dr. Andersen, Father Nelson made a different announcement:

"Dr. Andersen has just informed me that we have been quarantined."

Some of the big boys started to cheer, but they were silenced when Father Nelson's big hands, with all fingers spread, simultaneously and swiftly lowered a few, inches, sending the unmistakable sign to *sit down and listen, now*! He continued his speech.

Quarantined

"Dr. Andersen believes that several of our Tots have Scarlet Fever. It is a very contagious sickness. Those children will be kept in the infirmary upstairs until they are completely better. If anyone else gets sick, they will also go to the infirmary until they are completely well. Once there are no more *new* cases of the sickness here for a week, everyone who hasn't gotten sick can return to school."

There was no actual cheering, but the healthy, strong boys and girls who had been in the home for a while knew that if they weren't actually sick, there would be many days or weeks of one hundred percent play!

Christine looked at Doris, as if to check her reaction. Doris didn't look scared, or happy, or sick, or anything else. Doris, who had been able to handle getting all the Tots up and dressed this morning, and all the other unfamiliar and difficult things she had faced since they arrived at The Home, was now trying to figure out what had just happened, and what they would do next. Staring out the window, her mind wandered. Doris was thinking about when they lived in Elizabeth, and their mother told them they were quarantined. The boys had Chicken Pox. None of them went out to play, or to school. Not even Sunday School. After a few days, she and Christine also got the Chicken Pox, but the days before she and Christine got sick, there was a lot of play! Their mother hung sheets around the boys to keep the germs from spreading. Christine and Doris used the sheets as stage curtains and put socks over their hands to make puppets. They put on one show after another that made their brothers laugh and took their minds off the itching, at least for a while. She enjoyed the memories of Mamma putting them in a warm, soothing bath. Sometimes Mamma would just sit in the room with them and sew or knit, while they played. As she relived that experience and remembered the fun they had, she began to understand why some of the children wanted to cheer.

The happy memories were helpful, but Doris still had to overcome the disappointment she was feeling about missing school. All of her homework was done and ready to be passed in to Miss. Goodman. Since there was no hope of going to school, Doris decided that she would take some time today to read the next chapter in her books. This thought led her to the next; *maybe I could help Christine to do the same thing in her books, and practice writing with her right hand.* Her excitement grew and she thought, *maybe we could do those things and play at the same time. We could play school!* Okay. She now felt ready. Looking around she realized that the only children left in the dining room were the Hauklands and Nancy, and they were all looking at her, waiting for Doris to tell them what was going on, and what they were supposed to do next.

Miss Flotten had explained quarantine to Doris, so as clearly as she could, she explained it to her audience. "Being quarantined, means that no one from The Home can go to school, because some of the Tots here are very sick. What is making them sick is a germ that that can spread to others. Sometimes before people look and feel sick, they are silently getting sick. During the silent time, the germ can still go to other people, like the ones on the trolley, or our teachers or the other students. So, the rest of us can't go to school until the doctor is sure none of us are in the silent time. We will all stay here until no one else gets sick for a week. Then, the healthy ones go back to school and the sick ones stay in the infirmary until their bodies win the fight against the germ, and they are well again. Anyone who gets Scarlet Fever has to stay in the infirmary for forty days, so they don't get anyone else sick.

Right now, since we're not sick, we just get to play!" In almost the same breath, she asked the little group, "Do you want to play school?"

Nancy and Christine thought it was a good idea, but Oscar said, "No!" and Alert really wasn't expected to play school. Doris decided that with the majority of three, they would go to the playroom in the girls building and either use the classroom that Hazel had set-up, or make a new one.

Outside the brick building Oscar heard the bigger boys playing hockey on the ice rink. "Doris, can I go and watch the boys playing hockey?" he asked. Since that was his favorite thing to do, Doris agreed, but first she made sure his coat was buttoned all the way up, and his hat covered his ears.

The playroom was more crowded and noisy than it had been since they arrived there. It seemed like everyone, except the boys playing hockey had come to the playroom. The large playroom, now felt very small.

Christine said, "I don't like how it feels here." Nancy nodded her head in agreement, saving herself the effort of making herself heard over all the other children.

"Do you want to take a few things for Alert to play with, and go up and play in our room, and use our school books?" Doris asked.

Both girls agreed, and Alert wasn't especially concerned about his surroundings. As long as he had a few things to play with, he was content, any place.

Not having a black board and chalk made it less like school, but that was okay. Doris tried to be in charge like a teacher, but she was careful not to be too bossy. She didn't want her students to change their minds, and find something else more fun, than playing school with her.

Doris was surprised by her success as a teacher. Her students had done some math, some penmanship and they were still very engaged in reading from Nancy and Christine's reader, when the lunch bell sounded. Christine and Nancy were a little reluctant to stop reading, and they both actually said thank you to Doris, as they closed their books and left their new classroom. "You're welcome," Doris answered. "We can do this again tomorrow after breakfast, if you want to." Both girls agreed to this plan.

Alert was the most ready to go for lunch. He took Doris's hand and said, "Lets go." Doris was delighted with Alert's success in expressing himself.

Fortunately, none of the Hauklands or Nancy got Scarlet Fever. Several more of the Tots and a few of the bigger boys and girls did. Miss Flotten took care of the Tots during the night, and one of the older girls was taught what to do for them while she slept during the day. Miss Bersager and Miss Johnson took care of the older girls and boys, making separate infirmaries to isolate them.

Father Nelson had to call Pappa at Mrs. Boardsen's house, to tell him about the quarantine. Doris got to speak to him on the phone for just a minute, and he was glad to hear that all of the Hauklands (and Nancy) were healthy. "We miss you, Pappa. We can't wait 'til you come again," Doris said. Before he said goodbye Pappa reminded her that he would have to be at work the following Sunday, so he would be there the week after that, if the quarantine was lifted.

Chapter 18
Back to "Normal"

Finally, Dr. Andersen made his last visit for this particular illness. He told Father Nelson, that some of the children who had gotten Scarlet Fever would still be quarantined, but it would be all right if the children who hadn't gotten sick went back to school. The announcement at dinner that night didn't bring the happiness the quarantine announcement had. It had been four weeks since any of The Home kids had been to school.

Secretly, Doris was very happy. Her make-believe school with Christine and Nancy was fun, and they all made a lot of progress. Doris completed all of the lessons the class had done before she arrived, Nancy practiced reading out loud and Christine was writing with her right hand - almost without thinking about it. Doris and her students were ready to return to *real* school.

Miss Goodman made Doris feel very welcome, without making her feel embarrassed, on her first day back. Doris noticed that Miss Goodman's lessons really did build on material from the beginning of the books, and having reviewed all the lessons, helped her understand the new material better.

After school, Nancy and Christine told Doris that their teacher wanted to know who had taught them while they were absent. "Miss Braxton said you should be a teacher when you grow up," said Nancy.

"I'm going to be a nurse when I grow up, but I'm glad our make believe school helped you and Christine."

This coming Sunday, Pappa would finally be able to come to visit. He hadn't been able to visit for four weeks, because of the quarantine and his work schedule.

So many things had happened since Pappa's last visit. Lying next to Christine, in their clean nightgowns and sheet, after their bath on Saturday night, Doris tried to remember some of the things she wanted to tell Pappa when he came.

So much of what was new and exciting to them last time Pappa came, was now normal routine. Last time, they all wanted to speak at once. Now, Doris felt calmer, and pleasantly comfortable with the every-day life in The Home. She wondered if it was a bad thing that she didn't miss her old life with Mamma and Pappa in Elizabeth as much as she used to. She forced herself to think about each of her parents to make sure she still felt as much love for them, as she always had.

It was getting harder to remember what Mamma looked like, but when she thought of her, there was always so much love in her heart. Doris truly loved her mother, and she knew, right then and there, that she would never stop loving her mother. This made her feel freer to enjoy both the memories of her old home and the happiness she was feeling in her new Home.

Next, she forced herself to think of her Pappa. He was much easier to picture in her mind, because she saw him more recently. She thought for a minute about how thin and sad he looked ever since Mamma died, but her test worked for Pappa, too. There was so much love that would never go away. She thought of how proud he said he was about the things she was doing for the others in The Home, and how good it made her feel that she pleased him.

No, she decided. *Because I don't miss Mamma and Pappa every day, like I used to, isn't a bad thing. It is what would make them happy. It would make Pappa very sad if next time he came I told him that I missed him so much I just sat in the chair he sat in, except when it was time to eat, until he came again. What seemed to make him happy were the things I did to help my brothers and sister, and the others in The Home, and that I was happy.*

Just before she drifted off to sleep, Doris decided that even though she wasn't bursting with new things to tell Pappa, when he saw her and the others, he would see that they were all happy. He would know they weren't pretending, they really were happy. She thought she would tell Pappa more about Miss Flotten and all the Tots, and Miss Baker and Miss Goodman, and Dottie and Hazel and Nancy, and Miss Bersager, and then, without warning, she was asleep.

Pappa was there after Sunday Dinner, just as they hoped. The boys weren't dressed in the fancy suits they wore for his last visit. They had changed into play clothes right after Chapel was over. Oscar was much happier in play clothes, than he had been in that fancy suit. All four arrived in the entry room to find Pappa sitting near where he was standing for the last visit, and he had already pulled two other chairs close to the one he was sitting in.

Before climbing into their places, they all climbed onto as much of Pappa's lap as any four children could occupy at the same time. Pappa beamed as his long arms reached around and made a hug big enough to include all four of his children. *It is so good to see them. They look so healthy and happy,* he thought.

Rooted

This time there was no waiting to see what was in the brown paper bag. Oscar couldn't wait another second to see if there was a second hockey player. Sure enough, there was. Pappa had made this one with his cap tipped to the side, so Oscar would know which was which. When Oscar took the first player from his pocket, and held the two pieces together, Pappa was happy to see that the first player was now a different color from having been played with so much.

Doris and Christine got a little carved bat, and a wooden puck that they could step on a certain way to make it jump straight up, so they could hit it with the bat. Oscar liked that toy, too, and asked if next time he could have one of them. Pappa smiled, and said "Sure, but you'll all have to be careful that no one gets hurt when you play with it."

Oscar agreed.

Alert's toy was a car, just about the same size as the boat. The wheels didn't spin, but that wasn't a problem for him, he could move it along even without moving wheels.

It was the first weekend in March, but Pappa said, "It's so mild outside, why don't we go out and you can try your toys where there is room to play. I brought some peppermint patties and a few oranges and apples. If it's still warm enough after we play a little, we can sit on the porch bench. I'll peel the fruit and we can have a snack."

It felt like it had been a whole year of only winter, and the Hauklands were very happy to have the opportunity to be outside for a while. Pappa picked a spot on the lawn, where no one would be walking and the ground wasn't too muddy. He showed the children how the bat and puck worked. He was quite good at it. He made it look so easy that they were all eager to try.

They tried, and tried and tried again, but the puck just wouldn't jump up, and if it came up at all, it wasn't nearly high enough that they could hit it with the bat. They had seen that it did work for Pappa, so both girls continued to work at it, as Alert made believe the whole lawn was a big road for his new car.

Pappa and Oscar walked around to the back of the girls building, where Pappa sat on a rock that was the top step of a large rock stair case and he and Oscar flattened a little spot on the ground where there was no grass. They found a small, nicely rounded stone for a puck and made a little small hole on each side of their court to be the goal. Pappa was the new player, as Oscar had become very fond of the one he already had. They decided before they started that they would play until one of their players got 12 points. One each time the stone went into the opposite hole.

There was a lot of laughing and cheering as father and son played hard with the little figures. Before long Oscar's player had twelve points and Pappa's man had seven.

"Thank you, Pappa," Oscar said feeling very happy to have gotten that special time with his father, to have another carved hockey player and also because he was the winner. He put one of the men into each of his pant pockets as they walked, back around the building to meet the others.

Pappa was a little surprised that the girls were still working at trying to hit their pucks, and he was pretty sure he could already see a little improvement. "Good job, girls! Now, let's go in, wash our hands in the bathroom and come back out to have a piece of fruit before the sun goes down and it starts to get cold," Pappa said.

On the side and around the back of the girls building, there was a wide, covered porch. The only piece of furniture that was still on the porch in the winter was a glider. It was a long, metal seat that looked like an outside sofa, but without cushions. The glider rocked back and forth, if you made it, by pushing your feet into the floor, and straightening then bending your knees. Since none of them could make it glide, it just felt like a cold, shaky bench.

With all the Haukland children and their Pappa sitting on the glider, Pappa took the knife out of his pocket, and with as much accuracy and skill as he used to carve wooden things, he began at the top of an apple, and continued in a circular pattern, never breaking the band of skin, until he reached the bottom. Then he sliced wedges for each of his children, and handed them to each one between the flat side of the knife and his thumb.

Doris thought *I don't ever remember an apple tasting this good,* but all she said was, "Thank you, Pappa - for the apple and for our new toys."

The others joined in, "Thank you Pappa,"

This time Alert also managed to say, "Thank you, Pappa," instead of Ta Ta.

Father Nelson again asked Pappa if he would stay for a meal, and this time there was no hesitation. Pappa said, "Thank you very much, Father Nelson, I would be very happy to enjoy supper here.

Once again, Pappa sat in the staff dining room, next to Father Nelson, where he could see his family. Once, the girls thought Pappa was waving to them, but when they looked more closely, they realized that Pappa was spelling something with his fingers. "G-o-o-d s-a-n-d-w-i-c-h-e-s."

The signs were a little different than they ones they had been learning from the other kids, but it was still easy for them to understand Pappa. The girls giggled when they understood the message and answered back. "Y-e-s."

Having been nourished and warmed by the meal, and the joy of being with his children, Magnus prepared to leave for Brooklyn. "Do you have to leave already?" Christine asked.

"Yes, Christine, it's time for me to start back to *my* new home."

"When will you come again, Pappa?" Christine asked.

"I plan to come every other Sunday. It was longer than that this last time, because of the quarantine. Father Nelson called to tell me that no visitors were allowed until Dr. Andersen allowed the healthy children to return to school. I hope everyone will stay healthy, so we won't have to wait so long next time. Is there anything any of you want me to bring next time?"

Oscar reminded Pappa of his wish to have a puck and bat, and Christine said, "No, Pappa, I can't think of anything. Maybe another apple, that was very good!"

"Pappa," said Doris a little hesitantly. "Would you bring one of the pictures we used to have at home? I was thinking about Mamma, and I wanted to see her picture."

"Certainly, Doris, I will look through the ones I have and bring one to you. That is a good idea," Pappa answered.

Doris was relieved that Pappa wasn't upset by her request. She was always a little afraid to talk about Mamma to Pappa. She didn't want to make him sad all over again, especially right now, when he looked very happy.

Since it wasn't as cold this evening as it was the last time Pappa visited, they all decided to walk Pappa to the end of the road where he would catch the trolley.

Before they all left the brick building, Pappa found Father Nelson, and stopped briefly to shake his hand. "Thank you, Father Nelson. It is such a relief and a joy to see my children so happy. I plan to be back in two weeks. Good night."

Father Nelson stood up when Pappa went in the room to talk to him, and as usual, he put his left hand on Pappa's shoulder as he shook his right hand. "Have a safe trip home, Magnus. God bless you."

Doris, Oscar, Pappa, Alert and Christine all held hands as they walked down the street, and every few steps Alert would be swung up in the air, until the swingers were too tired. With minimal protesting, Alert kept his feet on the ground the rest of the way down the hill.

"Pappa, see trolley," Alert said, putting three words together, for the first time. The children stood by the side of the road and waved until they could no longer see Pappa and soon the trolley disappeared from their sight, also.

The sun had already gone down and darkness was filling in under the trees, as the children walked back up the hill. They all felt happy to have had their visit with Pappa, but were now comfortable to say goodbye and return to the big stone building, which they now knew as the girls's building, and the big brick building, which was called the boys's building. This was home - or as most people, like teachers and store keepers, the doctor and Father Nelson called it, The Home. And now, they had truly become Home Kids.

Chapter 19
Exploring Out Back

 $\mathcal{D}$ oris said, "Soon it will stay light even after supper, and it will be warmer outside, so we can explore the outside, just like we have explored the inside, here."

Oscar said, "The boys by the skating rink say that behind the girls's building there is a very big playground."

"Okay," said Doris, "if it's nice when Christine and I get home from school, tomorrow, let's all go down the steps behind the house, and see what's there."

"That sounds scary, Doris. It looks like the ground just drops straight down when I look out the window in the back. It looks like it goes all the way to the river without anything to stop you from falling," said Christine.

"That's what I thought, too, Christine," said Doris. "Tomorrow we will all go very carefully, and see for ourselves - before it gets dark, O.K?"

They all agreed to face this scary expedition together. Even Alert nodded his head. They all walked back to the boys's building, where they played for a while before getting Oscar and Alert settled into their beds.

Walking back to the girls building, Christine and Doris looked out toward the river. The lights from all of the buildings in New York City sparkled like nothing they had ever seen before. It was beautiful, but it surely didn't do anything to help them believe what the big boys said about a playground behind the girls building.

When the girls met after class, Christine said, "Doris, I told Nancy about our exploring adventure this afternoon, and she wants to know if she can come, too?"

"Of course she can. Nancy is always welcome with us," said Doris.

Christine and Doris loved going to school. With the warmer days, their trip to and especially from school was a lot more pleasant. Not only was it brighter, now they didn't have to worry about sliding on the snow or ice, either. They especially appreciated that today, when they were hurrying to meet up with their brothers to go exploring. The three girls brought their books up to their room, and changed to play clothes.

One quick stop was made before calling for the boys in their building. The girls had learned something interesting during the quarantine. They knew the kitchen was on the first floor of their building, past the room with the piano, and the nurses's dining room. Their noses and the cooking noises that came from there told them that's where the meals were prepared. That explained the big boys carrying those huge pots over to the dining room in the boys's building before every meal.

What they had learned by watching the other children during the quarantine was that in the kitchen, there was a big closet, called a pantry. The men who worked at The Home would drive to the local stores in the evenings. The store owners were happy to have them collect all of the bread, muffins, cookies, rolls and cup cakes that were still left on the shelves at the end of the day, to make room for the fresh delivery the next morning. The men brought the leftover bakery things to The Home, and arranged them on the shelves in the pantry. The children were allowed to go there after school, and take anything they wanted for snacks!

The three girls each chose cupcakes for themselves and they brought one for each of the boys. They all sat in the dining room in the brick building and ate their snacks. It took a little patience to wait for Oscar and Alert to peel the tightly folded paper away from the soft, sweet, moist cupcakes with the chocolate icing and finish eating. Then, they had to hunt up a damp rag, take the chocolate icing off their brothers and get their coats on.

The brave explorers first discovery was, instead of having to hold onto the porch railings and walk single file along a narrow path, as they had imagined, there was a nice wide path behind the building. This was a good start, but the ground really did drop off on the side of the path away from the building, and there was no fence to prevent them from falling off the edge. They walked in twos, staying closer to the building, with Doris leading them. There were trees where the ground dropped off, but they only saw the tops of them from the path.

When they walked about halfway around the back of the girls building, on their left side was an opening, with a very wide piece of flat rock on the ground. Oscar said, "This is where Pappa and I played hockey with my wooden men."

This rock made the top landing. Another large rock made the next step, then another big flat stone made a second landing. If they continued to walk straight ahead, there wasn't another step. The ground just dropped off. The ground also dropped off to the right side of the second landing, but on the left side there was another very big flat stone that made another step. This continued, with every step a different shape and width and length.

They continued to go down the steps. Since the trees were still mostly without leaves, they could begin to see what looked like a large, flat area to the right, below them. They kept going down, stepping with caution. Alert had a little trouble with any steps, so this was especially challenging for him.

Some of the steps were angled up or down and some were large and square, like another landing. A few times, instead of going straight down, they had to walk sideways on hard dirt. Each step took a lot of concentration, so they weren't able to look down at what they were thinking might be the playground the big boys were talking about.

Near the bottom, there were no more steps, but they continued to go further downward on sloping, bare-dirt ground. Now, instead of being helpful, rocks were sticking up like traps. They were different sizes and shapes and were coming out of the ground at all angles. They were far enough apart to walk between them, but there was no definite path. Doris was afraid that if any of them tripped on one of the rocks, they would fall and hit their heads on the next one.

The explorers used extreme caution navigating this area. Finally, ah, they had made it. Now, they could stand on relatively level ground and look around them. This was bigger than any park they had ever seen! All around it was a very tall chain-linked fence that was set into concrete posts.

"WATCH OUT!" They heard from behind. The explorers scurried to the side, and as she turned, Doris grabbed Alert and pulled him out of the way of three boys who were *flying* down so fast that it looked like they were even skipping some of the steps!

All five explorers stood there, shocked that anyone could come down those crazy steps that fast. Then it happened again. This time it was four boys. They seemed to know each step, and their feet touched down so surely and swiftly that they could just as easily have been running across a grassy field with no obstacles.

"That is amazing!" Nancy said. "How can they do that?"

"I don't know," answered Doris, "but I bet that some day, we will, too."

Looking across the grassy ground with some very big and some smaller rocks protruding here and there, they saw several groups of swings, a seesaw and two slides; one tall and one short, and a cute little house that looked like a life-sized doll house.

Looking through the fence on the riverside from where they were standing, there was nothing to see but the sky. When they walked a little closer to the fence, they could see the very tops of some trees, and when they bravely stood right at the fence, putting their hands through the spaces and wrapping their fingers around the cold, strong wire, they could see all the way down to the river. Across the river, they could see the tall buildings that were being built in Manhattan, and realized where the pounding noises they had been hearing were coming from.

They watched ferry boats crossing from beneath them over to Manhattan, and there were some larger ships moving up and down the river, too. From where they were standing, the tall buildings didn't look very big. They could also see that almost straight down, there were houses that were all in a row, right near the water. They looked so tiny that the children weren't sure they were real houses.

By now, there were already a few children on the

swings. In Elizabeth, some of the swings had little boxes for the babies. Here there were only flat metal seats. Christine and Nancy found two empty swings next to each other, and started to pump. Alert was sitting on one of the larger rocks, a safe distance from the swings, playing with his toy boat. Doris helped Oscar onto one of the swings. She told him to hold the chains tightly; then she backed up a few steps, pulling the swing with her. Oscar's eyes widened as he felt like he was going to fall backward. Then she let it go, so he swung backwards. Standing in front of him, she used his knees to give him a gentle push when he swung back toward her. Nothing about the expression on his face told Doris that he was enjoying the swing, so she didn't push him again. Sure enough, while he was still holding the chains, Oscar slid off the metal seat. He was able to reach the ground with his toes, and he dragged them on the dirt until he stopped.

When he started to walk away, she took him by the shoulders and directed him out past where the other swings would reach. She explained that it was very important not to walk in front or in back of the swings while someone was on them. Oscar didn't particularly like being lectured by his big sister, especially where there were other boys around, but Doris realized this was both new and serious and she hoped the lesson got through to him.

Without asking or telling anyone what he was going to do, Oscar found a quiet, flat spot on the ground, to play. He used the flat side of his hands to smooth out the dirt and a stick he found a short distance away to gouge a hole on each side of the newly constructed hockey rink, to make the goals. It wasn't that he wanted to play alone, but he didn't want anyone else to accidentally break his little wooden figures, and right now, on his first day in this playground, he really didn't want to play with Alert or the girls.

Doris took Alert on one of the swings. She held him on her lap with one hand, as she gently swung, holding the cold chain with her other hand. Even though they weren't going high, she could feel him lose his breath the first few times they went forward. Doris inhaled deeply, enjoying the clean fresh air, and said to Alert, "Isn't it fun to be outside, playing?"

She could feel his head moving up and down against her chest, but this time she just smiled and let him get away without speaking. Alert didn't seem to want to stop swinging, but Doris wanted to try the slides.

Doris let Alert climb up the steps right in front of her, then she pulled him onto her lap and they slid down together. Each time they went down Doris would say "whee," and by the third time, when Doris forgot, Alert filled the air with the sound of his own "whee!"

It must have looked and sounded like fun, because Oscar was lured from his hockey game to give the slides a try. He started with the little slide, and when he found he could do it completely by himself, he kind of reluctantly asked if Doris would stand at the bottom of the big slide while he came down. By the third time, he learned to push his feet out against the sides to slow himself down toward the bottom and to keep his feet under him when he landed. From then on, he was on his own.

Nancy and Christine had checked out the inside of the dollhouse and they decided that next time they would bring their dolls to play house. After that, they were running all over the playground, playing tag. After the slide, Alert and even Oscar ran around, trying to catch Nancy and Christine. Doris, who also joined the games, enjoyed watching them run and hearing them laugh. In fact, as she watched all the children in the playground she felt that, like her, they were all exceptionally happy to be playing outside!

It was starting to get a little cold and dark, and Doris was concerned about getting up those steps if it got any darker, so she gathered the explorers and they cautiously made their way up the steps, occasionally being passed by one of the veterans.

Dinner was warm and good, but Alert didn't even make it to dessert before he fell asleep in his high chair. The older girls who were walking around the dining room, bringing food and helping the younger children, laughed as they saw his little head lying on his high chair tray. Doris finished her dinner, then carried him up stairs, took off his play clothes and put on his night diapers, (which were still dry most mornings, now), rubber pants, and pajamas, all without him waking up.

Oscar, who made it through dessert, was also ready to sleep earlier than usual. By the time Doris, Christine and Nancy got to their homework, they had to force themselves to stay awake until it was finished. The fresh air and all the extra activity had brought them all a healthy readiness for sleep.

When Doris met Alert in the corner of his crib the next morning, he spit out his home-made pacifier and said, "whee!"

Doris laughed as she lifted him out and explained, hoping he was able to understand; "First Doris and Christine have to go to school. When we get home, if it is warm and not raining, we will go back to the playground."

The day at school went fast, but when the girls picked up their snacks and got to the boys, Alert wasn't interested in his cupcake. "Whee" he said again, pulling Doris toward the door.

Miss Flotten who was walking through the Tots's room said, "Dukken, Alert and I have been waiting for you all day. He kept looking out the window and saying, "Go Whee." I tried to interest him in trucks or a book, but he wouldn't even play with Oscar. Doris laughed as she told Miss Flotten about their expedition to the playground, yesterday.

"Ah," Miss Flotten said, "Now I understand. Why don't you take his cupcake down there and let him have a picnic."

Oscar agreed to the change in plans and they all carefully worked their way back to the playground for their second day of fresh air and the freedom to run and play in the biggest playground ever. Right now, none of them were overly impressed by the panoramic view from their park, looking out over the Hudson River and the New York City skyline.

The playground became a daily destination. Alert finally gave in and played with Oscar in the morning, but after his nap, he was back at the window waiting for the girls. Down in the playground, they'd have a quick snack sitting on a large rock, then running free and playing on the slide, and swings or the seesaw, and in the little house, until they heard the dinner bell.

They had never had so much freedom to play outdoors. In Elizabeth, there was only the space between their step and the curb in the front and in the back there was a very small over-grown, grassy yard, which rarely saw sunshine because of all the houses around it. Doris couldn't imagine any place that could be better than this.

Chapter 20
West Park

School was almost over for the year. Next year, Christine would be in the second grade, Doris would be a fourth grader, and Oscar would start kindergarten. The girls both liked their teachers a lot and were sad to think of not having the same ones again, but they also didn't want to be left back, so they would gladly accept that change. The change that Doris had been trying to avoid thinking about since she first heard of it on her second day at The Home, was West Park - some called it camp.

Whatever they called it, she couldn't go anywhere without hearing kids talking about it. The things they said didn't sound inviting to her, but whenever anyone talked about it, they looked so happy and excited, that even though Doris couldn't imagine why any of the children would ever want to go someplace else to play for the summer, she had to admit, there must be something special about it.

Today, that wasn't the most important thing to think about, though. Today was a Pappa Sunday and he was already on his way to visit them. They were eager to see him, again. Although he had planned to come every other Sunday, he had missed several visits because he was sick, and he still had to go to work on the alternate Sunday's, so he couldn't switch the days he would visit.

Pappa's visit after their first introduction to the park, had been on a rainy day, and because the trees were beginning to sprout their leaves, he couldn't even see the swings or the slide from the top of the steps. Today they had a secret plan to bring him down to the playground with them. Pappa always brought fruit and candy, and they had decided to have a picnic in the playground. Now he would get to be there with them and see how beautiful it was and all the things they could do down there.

His four children, and Nancy, who was now like one of his own, were sitting on the porch waiting to see Pappa come walking up the hill. But instead, someone had given him a ride in their car. Pappa stepped out of the big black car and as he closed the door, he bent over and said, "Thank you very much," to the driver.

When he turned to come up the porch steps, the children ran to greet him. The younger children didn't seem to notice, but Doris thought Pappa was moving much more slowly than usual. Even before he missed the last few visits, Doris had noticed that he was breathing funny, and sometimes he would stop playing for a moment and put his hand on his chest, then he'd start to play again. She had asked if he was all right, and he said he was fine. Now she was wondering if Pappa really was fine.

He still had the little paper bag, and he greeted all five children with a hug. The children didn't even want him to settle on the glider. They were determined to bring him to the playground. They told him they had a surprise for him, and asked him to come with them. They walked on the porch, to the back of the building, then went down just a few wooden porch steps to the big flat stone that made the top landing. Doris couldn't wait for Pappa to see how fast she could go down the uneven, stone steps, but as they all stood at the top of the steps, Pappa said, "I'm so sorry, children, but I can't go down all of those steps."

"What's the matter, Pappa?" asked Doris.

"You know I have been sick, and my body still isn't as strong as it was. I'm afraid that even if I get down all those tricky steps, I won't be strong enough to get back up."

Magnus could see the disappointment in all of the children's faces, and it brought on an ache in his heart that was just as hard for him to accept as the physical pains he was now having on a regular basis. "Maybe next time, I will be stronger," he said, trying to sound a lot more hopeful than he was.

Doris quickly said, "Christine, will you and Nancy go to the pantry and get a few cookies for us to have with our fruit, and you can meet us back on the glider. Oscar, do you want to help the girls choose a snack?"

"Okay," all three answered.

Alert persisted; "Go whee, go whee," attempting to pull Doris toward the steps.

"Alert," Doris said trying to distract him, "Oscar,  Christine and Nancy have gone to get cookies for us, and we're going to sit on the porch with Pappa and have our treats."

Pappa was grateful for Doris's ability to get him out of the uncomfortable situation, and he seemed relieved to sit back in the glider with Alert and Doris. Pappa reached inside his coat and handed Doris a large, rectangular envelope. Doris loved surprises from

Pappa. She had forgotten that she asked him to bring a picture of Mamma.

Opening the envelope, she exclaimed, "Pappa, thank you! This is my favorite picture. I love how Mamma is holding my hand here, when I was a baby. Thank you for remembering."

Pappa took this time to tell Doris that he planned to see the doctor this coming week. He said to this not-yet-nine-year-old, young woman, "I hope the doctor will be able to give me something that will help me get stronger. I have been able to keep working as a night watchman, because I am able to sit a lot. Every two hours I have to walk around the building, look around at everything and then slide a key into special clocks in a few different places, to show I was there and everything was all right. Then I can sit again. I find the trip here is a lot harder. I was very glad to get a ride up the hill this afternoon. I hope that before too long, I will be able to go down to the playground with all of you."

In her heart, when her Pappa said he was going to the doctor, Doris was suddenly afraid that Pappa was going to die, too. She knew the others would be back soon, and she didn't want them to see her cry; besides, if she cried, Pappa would feel a lot worse. Pappa said he hoped he would get better soon, so she decided she had to be brave, and hope with him, and pray that he would soon get better.

She bravely said, "Thank you for coming today, even though it was so hard for you, and thank you for remembering the picture. Pappa, we are doing well here. But there is one thing that I don't know about. All of the children are talking about going away to a camp, called West Park, soon. They say that we will go there right after school is over for the year and stay there until school starts again in September. They say no busses or trolleys go there, so I don't know how you could come to visit us in the summer?"

"I am sorry, Doris. I had forgotten all about that," said Pappa. "When I first spoke with Father Nelson, many months ago, he talked about a camp that is in New York State where the children go to spend the summer. You are right. There is no transportation that would bring me there. I will have to work at getting stronger while you are all away at camp."

Pappa continued, "Doris, you are such a blessing to our family. I know that your mother is watching from Heaven and she is very proud of you, just like I am. You are doing exactly what Mamma asked you to do. You are keeping our family together. All of the others look so happy, and I can see that they all look to you to watch over them. You are an amazing young lady, Doris."

That was all they could say before the others returned with cookies bulging in the pouch they made by pulling the bottom of Oscar's shirt up over itself. They all squeezed onto the glider, and divided up the cookies. Pappa used his little knife to pare the skin off an apple, without a single break in the peel, and cut it into little pieces, just the right size for their little mouths.

Even though they were sitting so close to the steps that brought them into what felt like a fairyland to the children, no one mentioned the playground for the rest of the afternoon. They talked about school, Nancy's aunt and cousins, the older boys playing a different game with a ball and a stick, in the field next to where the hockey rink was before it melted, and they talked of everything each of them had heard about the camp they would be going to soon.

When Pappa noticed the same man who had given him a ride up the hill, walking toward his car in front of the building, he called to him. "Excuse me, could I impose on you for a ride back down the hill?" Pappa asked.

"It would be a pleasure," the man answered, "I'll bring the car around here in just a minute."

Pappa gave each of the children a hug, and a nickel. He said, "Hold onto this, and if you have a place to buy a treat near the camp, you can spend it. I will write to you while you are at camp. I hope you all have a lot of fun there. When you get back to the Home, I hope I will be stronger, so we'll be able to go down to the playground."

The man brought his car right to the porch entrance and he opened the door for Pappa. The five children stood on the porch and waved, as Pappa rode down the hill with his arm out the window, still waving, until he was out of sight.

Doris asked the others to wait while she ran up the stairs and put her picture in the box, with her doll clothes, under the bed. The children seemed to sense that something was wrong, but none of them said anything more about Pappa's visit.

As they didn't mind going down and up the tricky steps to the playground, they decided that even though it would be only a few minutes until supper, they would still like to go there. Doris held Alert's hand on the steps, but once they reached the bottom, he was on his own - his first choice? "Go whee!"

The heaviness that Doris had been feeling in her chest somehow lifted as she ran behind Alert to the short slide. She kept her hands close behind him, just in case he tripped going up the ladder, and lightly held him by one arm as he rounded the last step and sat himself on the top of the slide where he waited while she ran to the bottom of the slide. There, she looked into his eyes and smiled, enjoying his expression for the few seconds it took him to reach the bottom. As he slowed down, she tucked her hands under his arms, lifted him off the slide and twirled around three times before returning him to the ground to repeat, and repeat, and repeat what had become his favorite thing.

Doris came close to crying about Pappa's illness, and the thought of not seeing him until after the summer, but she didn't give in to it. She continued to hope that he would get better. Every night, Doris would pray that her father would get better.

For as long as she could remember, Doris spoke often to God. Not just when she went to bed, or in the morning. Sometimes, it would be because she felt so very happy that she couldn't keep from saying thank you to God, and sometimes, like when Mamma died, or when Pappa told her he was sick, it was because she was so sad that it hurt. Sometimes, it was just that she wanted to talk to God about the things she was doing. She loved that He was always with her. Doris's mother had taught her about God, and how much He loves her. Their Mamma used to read stories and verses from the Bible to all the children.

The last day of school for the year, which was really only a half-day, was exciting for many reasons. In addition to being Doris's last day in the third grade, it was also the last morning she would wake up at The Home in Fort Lee until the summer was over. This would be the day she would see, with her own eyes, the camp in West Park, NY, that she had heard so much about. So many times, she had tried to envision what each of the other Home Kids had told her about their experiences there, but it was just too hard to imagine it all.

She wasn't sure what a creek was. She remembered the dirty, muddy water under the bridge they lived near, in Elizabeth. When she described that creek to any of the Home Kids, and asked "is that what the creek is like?" The kids laughed and said, "NO!" When she asked if it looked like the river they saw from the playground, again, they said "NO!"

West Park

Asking questions wasn't helping her picture this camp, but she still wondered; *Would the big grassy field they talked about look like the playground they had come to love so much? There probably wouldn't be the tall fence around this field, and surely there wouldn't be a view of New York City. What would it be like to not have any water in the bathroom sink, no bathtub, not even a real toilet? What would a farmhouse look like? What was it about the outhouse that made everyone giggle when they talked about it? What did it mean that there was room for three to use the bathroom at the same time? Why would any three people want to sit in an outside, tiny bathroom, without a real toilet?*

After devotions at breakfast, Father Nelson spoke about the bus trip. "The ride will take about two hours. Make sure that you bring anything you will want to have with you for the summer, because you won't be back here until the beginning of September - that is two months from now."

That sounded so final, so far away. Pappa said he would write to them while they were at camp, and he showed Doris how she could write to him. That helped a lot. Doris had already packed Pappa's address and he promised to send her a package with stamps and envelopes once they got settled in West Park.

Each of the Home Kids got a little cardboard box to pack their things in. Doris and Christine packed their shoeboxes including their little dolls and some clothes for them. Doris had her picture, and they all had the little wooden toys their father had made for them. Doris tried to imagine how empty the Fort Lee buildings would be without a single Home Kid there.

Twelve o'clock noon, on the last Friday in June, Doris gave her third grade teacher, Miss Goodman a hug before she left the classroom, and told her she would really miss her. She didn't say this to Miss Goodman, but she felt awful grown-up to be going into the fourth grade! This also meant that she would move into the middle bedroom in the girls building when they returned from camp. Over the summer, she would turn nine!

As they began their hike up the steep hill at The Home for the last time until after the summer, they saw three big busses lined up in front of the girls's building. She knew they were waiting to load every single Home Kid, and their treasures, and bring them up the parkway to this mysterious camp. Doris fought hard to quiet that now too familiar feeling she got when she had to accept things she was unhappy with or unsure about. Things she couldn't decide for herself.

She and her brothers and sister were going to camp. There was nothing she could do or say that would keep them from boarding that bus with all the other children. The only thing left for her to do, was to accept what was happening and make adjustments inside herself that would allow her to be happy, regardless of what she was facing. She decided to say - *that's just the way it is*, and trust that God would take care of them.

1923 School Bus

Chapter 21
Real Live Country

The bus ride was fun! Not like when they rode a trolley or bus in the city and didn't know anyone else on the bus. Here, they knew every face on the bus, and each of those faces looked exceptionally happy, today. There would be no more school for two months, and whatever the Hauklands would find at West Park, those who had been there before were very happy to be going back! There was singing and cheering and occasionally something would fly from one end of the bus to the other.

No longer on the parkway, the streets got narrow and there were a lot of sharp turns. Doris wondered why the driver didn't slow down, as all the kids first on one side then the other would scream and clutch the seat in front of them to keep from falling out into the aisle.

Whew, Doris thought when the bus finally slowed almost completely before making the last and sharpest turn. The bus drove right under a big iron archway with words written across the top. It said, "Christian Orphan Home…" but before she could finish reading the sign, they had passed under it and were riding on dirt! The bus kept going, slowly, rocking from side to side on the uneven ground, before it stopped on a grassy field between two hills. There were lots of trees; beautiful, tall trees full of fresh, light green leaves that left only the smallest spaces for the bright blue sky to be seen.

Kids were standing on the seats, and leaning over each other to get their first glimpses of camp. Doris could see a few buildings placed here and there up in the hills. They were all painted white with dark roofs. Some were so tiny that she couldn't imagine how even one bed could possibly fit in them.

The bus stopped and the doors opened. Doris kept trying to see outside, as the line of excited children inched slowly past her toward the exit door. She watched through the window as some of the children stood in the middle of the field with their arms outstretched and twirled around, drinking in the beautiful, green and blue picture. She wondered if what they were doing was a kind of celebration of being free – no more school or homework or traveling to and from school for the whole summer. She tried to remember having that feeling, and it took her back to twirling and dancing in their flat while her Mamma sang and clapped her hands for her.

Suddenly, her thoughts were interrupted. It was her turn to get off the bus. She jumped down the last, high step, set her box on the ground, then went back and lifted Alert down, and watched to see that Oscar, Nancy and Christine each jumped down without difficulty.

The trees looked so lush and she was surprised that the air here smelled even fresher than at The Home, in Fort Lee. West Park did look and feel different. There were no fences. It felt like there was no end to it. No big buildings in the distance, no noise from construction, no boats on the river. This was definitely different. Doris thought this must be what it means in stories when it talks about being in the country.

She couldn't think of one word that would describe it. It wasn't fancy; the buildings were plain white wooden buildings with dark roofs. It wasn't beautiful, like the well-groomed gardens full of brightly colored flowers they passed on their way to school. It was plain, peaceful, maybe even pretty, but not in a way that was made that way by someone trying to make it pretty. No, it looked more like the way it would have been if no one did anything except cut the grass, so children could play there, and placed a few buildings here and there in the woods, to make a place to sleep, eat, and play in, if it rained. So, just that quickly, the uneasy feeling in her stomach left and Doris decided *the children were right, this does look like a wonderful place to be.*

It was also quiet. More than just sounding quiet, it felt quiet. The only noise, which at the moment was quite loud, were children cheering and calling out to each other. They were happy sounds.

"Bobby, come on up here so you can get the bed next to mine."

"Anna, you'll be in this building, now - come on, I'll show you where to go."

"Bruce - did you bring the baseballs?"

It was all about getting settled in this new place and getting ready for lots of play.

Doris really wasn't sure where to go. She did know one thing; that she and Christine both needed to find the bathroom. Miss Bersager, Miss Flotten, and the other grown ups were in a car that was behind the buses, and they still hadn't arrived. Out of necessity more than courage, Doris asked one of the older girls where the bathroom was. Almost giggling, she pointed to one of the very small white houses Doris had seen on the hill.

"That's the bathroom?" asked Doris.

"Yes," answered the older girl. "Here it's called an outhouse. There isn't any water to flush the toilets here. When you use the bathroom, it goes down into a big hole in the ground. You'll see when you get there."

"Okay, thanks," said Doris, eager for relief. "Christine, run ahead and you can go first," she said gathering Oscar and Alert with her as she started up the hill.

"Hey Doris," Christine called from inside the little wooden house, "You can come in, too. There are three seats in here!"

Leaving the boys outside the door, Doris joined Christine. The first thing she noticed in the dim light was not what she saw or didn't see. It was the smell. It smelled awful! But right now that wasn't as important as being there. "Ah," she said with relief. "Do you think we'll get used to this smell, Christine?"

"I guess so," she answered. "It's kind of fun to finally be at camp. It's really beautiful here Doris, isn't it?"

"Yes," answered Doris, trying to do what she needed to, quickly, and get out of the smelly little house.

When they were finished, Doris sent Oscar and Alert in, telling Oscar to help his little brother. The air that smelled clean and fresh when they first got out of the bus, was even sweeter and cleaner, now that they had left that little house!

"Christine! Doris!" Nancy called, as she waved frantically from the door of one of the bigger buildings right near the outhouse. "Come on! All the beds are being taken! I am trying to hold three of them that are together for us."

"Good job," said Christine, trying to decide which of the three she wanted for herself. They all decided that Doris should be in the top bunk, which left two lower bunks, one for Christine who chose to be under Doris, and Nancy would be under another girl, but no one had claimed that upper bunk, yet.

The room was very large and filled with bunk beds. It felt cool, and smelled like damp wood. It seemed very dark when they first came in from outside, but before they had time to be concerned about that, their eyes adjusted, and it wasn't a problem. The room had little windows that were close to the ceiling, which wasn't really a ceiling, but just the inside of the roof.

The windows didn't slide up and down to open. They pushed out from the bottom and stayed attached on the top. Doris watched as some of the big girls pushed the little square windows out, and placed a stick between the window and the frame, to hold it open so they could get some fresh air into the room. All the windows had screens inside of them, and there was a solid wooden door that was propped open and a separate screen door, that opened with a squawk and closed with a loud bang.

With their boxes on their beds, as a sign to others that they were taken, the girls decided to hunt for the house that the tots would be in. Before she stepped off the little wooden steps of their building, Doris paused long enough to take in the view from this far up one side of the hill. The buses looked kind of small as they drove back out through the iron archway. With the buses gone, there would be no way to get back to Fort Lee, but even in the short time they were there, Doris had already decided this was where she wanted to be.

They would have to get back down to the field at the bottom of the hill to find out which one was the Tots's house. Doris was suddenly and pleasantly struck by the realization that she could decide for herself whether she would walk or run, or be quiet or let out a scream. Even with the extra weight and responsibility of carrying Alert, she chose to both run and scream.

Bursting with energy and happiness, Doris ran down the hill. Alert happily joined her in the scream, which changed tone as they bounced with each step. Doris was amazed at how hard it was to keep herself from going faster with each step. She loved the feeling of the breeze in her hair, and she had never felt so free.

Oscar tagged along behind the girls. He was starting to feel sleepy, but when they left the girls's building, he realized that he had mostly been getting tired of watching the girls get settled and bored by the things the girls were finding interesting.

Coming down off the hill he spotted something that made his day. It wasn't hockey, but there was a ball and lots of boys, and it was a game! Like Doris, he too had the chance to choose. Did he want to keep following the girls around to see where he and Alert would sleep or go and find out what those boys were playing? Oscar chose to check out the game. "See 'ya," he called back over his shoulder, as he ran down the hill, to the big, open field.

Doris and Alert met Dottie at the bottom of the hill, and she pointed out the dining room and the laundry building next to it. She said, "See that staircase on the side of the laundry? Go up those stairs, and you will be in the Tots's room."

"Thanks, Dottie," she said. Then, still carrying Alert, Doris ran up the hill toward the laundry, then up the steps. At the top step, she was totally out of breath. Both she and Alert were happy to be met by Miss Flotten, who showed them where Alert would sleep. Doris found Alert's little box in a corner with the other Tots's boxes. She and Alert unpacked his few possessions and set them up in and around the crib, to make him feel at home.

Doris asked Miss Flotten where Oscar would sleep, so she could reassure Alert that his brother would still be near him.

"Oscar won't be with the Tots any more, Dukken. Because he turned five, he will be with the boys, now."

Doris knew Alert would not be able to understand how important it was for Oscar to graduate from being one of the Tots. Alert knew all the other Tots well by now, so she made a game of telling him, that Freddy and Bobby and Thomas and Gustav and Emma and Anna and all the other Tots would still be in his room at night.

At the bottom of the hill, Oscar ran right to the closest boy he could find, and said, "What 'cha 'playin'?"

"Baseball," the boy answered, with a hint of impatience at Oscar's ignorance.

"We play it all summer," the boy added. "We have teams and we play each other."

"Is it like hockey?" asked Oscar.

"Naw," said the boy. Then he patiently took a little twig and using it as a pencil, drew a baseball diamond in the dirt. He explained the whole game to Oscar, who took in every word the boy told him, not missing one thing along the way.

A very loud, but pleasant clang came from a bell in front of a building that the experienced Home Kids knew was the dining room. Every bat and ball was dropped and the players all ran to the dining room. Kids streamed out of every building, all going in the same direction.

"Come on," said Oscar's new coach. "It's lunch time! My name is Bruce, what's yours?"

"My name is Oscar," he replied.

"Okay if I just call you Os?" the boy asked.

"I'd like that," Oscar replied. "Can I sit with you, at lunch?"

"Sure," said Bruce.

When they got to the table, Bruce introduced Os to the others. They all welcomed him, even though he was the youngest boy at the table.

Chairs scraped on the wooden floor as everyone hustled to get the seat of their choice. Doris and Alert had been in the next building over, so they were two of the earliest to arrive for lunch. They saved seats for Christine, Nancy and Oscar at their table.

Nancy and Christine arrived next, but when Oscar arrived, he walked right past the table without even noticing them. Oscar was busy talking to Bruce. Doris was very happy for Oscar when she saw him walk in with one of the bigger boys, and settle at his table.

A girl about Doris's age was one of the last to arrive in the dining room. When she asked if she could sit in the empty seat, Nancy, Christine and Doris all said she was welcome to join them. The girl looked kind of sad, and Doris was eager to talk to her, but Father Nelson was about to speak, so Doris would have to wait to introduce herself and the others.

With everyone seated, Father Nelson began. "Welcome to the summer of 1923 in West Park. Let's take a minute to give thanks for the food, and some of our blessings: We thank you, Father, for the safe trip and the opportunity to spend another summer in West Park. We ask your safety on each and every child throughout the summer. Help us all to remember that we are to enjoy our stay here, and to respect our neighbors and their property as well. We ask your blessing on the food that has been prepared for us. In Jesus's name, we pray, Amen."

The same girls who brought out the food in the dining room at The Home, brought out plates of peanut butter and jelly sandwiches. Doris introduced herself to the girl who sat in the seat they had saved for Oscar, and found out her name was Mary. The children all ate quietly, until they were satisfied, then waited to be dismissed, just as they had done in Fort Lee. It all felt so good to Doris - even the peanut butter and jelly sandwiches tasted better here.

Doris noticed that Mary didn't eat much, and she looked like she was going to cry a few times during the meal. Once Father Nelson told the kids they were dismissed, Doris introduced her to Christine, Nancy and Alert but she barely smiled at them. Doris remembered seeing her playing happily with another girl in Fort Lee, and thought maybe her friend was sick, or they weren't friends anymore, but before there was time to say any more to her, Mary had left the dining room.

Doris brought Alert to the Tots's room above the laundry for his nap. Miss Flotten had a room near the Tots, just like she did in Fort Lee. Alert was tired, but he wouldn't stay in his crib like he would when they were in Fort Lee. He cried and said, "No go Sissa."

Doris was so eager to continue to explore every building in the camp, and to see what was in the woods. She heard that there were paths through the woods that went to little houses where families spent their summers. Someone said there were two girls about the same age as Doris in one of the houses. She wondered if they would like to play with her. She wanted to see the nut trees and the bushes with wild berries that the children were allowed to pick and eat. One of the boys told Oscar that there was a place in the woods where a lot of trees had fallen, and the boys had made a little house they called a 'lean-to' with the trees. Every one of the Home Kids that spoke about the camp spoke about the creek, and Doris wanted to see where and what that was. Doris wanted to see it all.

Once again, she had a choice to make. She could sit by her brother while he took his nap, or she could trick him and once he fell asleep, she could go out and explore. Doris decided quickly, and assured Alert she would stay right by his crib while he slept. She got a book from Miss Flotten, made herself comfortable on the floor next to his crib, and read, while Alert slept. Doris understood that Alert had been through many, many changes in the last few months, and she chose to stay with him, at least for his nap, today. *Besides*, she told herself, *today is only the first day here. I have all summer to explore. Maybe I'll even find someone who has been a home kid for a long time, who will go with me to explore.*

Doris hadn't even finished the book when Alert stood up in the corner of his crib, looking for her. "I see you," she called to Alert, so he would look for her on the floor. Alert beamed when he saw his sister. *That smile*, Doris thought, *made it all worthwhile.* Doris spent the rest of the afternoon exploring with Alert. They found Christine and Nancy under a big shade tree, playing dolls. Nancy looked frustrated. She was not used to playing outside with her doll. Since Doris's doll was the same size as Christine's, Nancy asked Doris, "Could I use your doll, today?"

"Sure, Nancy, I'm not playing with him now. He's still in my box on the bed."

"Thanks, Doris, I'll be careful with him," she promised.

Next, they found Oscar or Os as he was now called, at the baseball field. There was a little bench on the side of the field, so Alert and Doris sat to watch the action. Alert seemed to enjoy watching the boys play. Os seemed to have several jobs. If a ball was hit too far for anyone else to get, Os ran for it, and put it back in play. When his team was up at bat, he became the official go-fer. Not really a catcher, because he wasn't allowed to stand close behind the batter, but when the ball got past the batter, he would go after it, and return it to the batter, who would throw it back to the pitcher.

Os couldn't have been happier. Since he first went to The Home, he had been watching the bigger boys play hockey. Now he wasn't just watching, they were letting him be part of a team!

After they watched for a while, Doris spotted a ball that wasn't being used. "Whose ball is this?" Doris called, when the teams were changing positions on the field. "It's mine," Andrew answered - "you can play with it."

"Thanks," Doris said, then she took the ball and Alert far enough from the ball field to be safe and not interfere with the game. Alert seemed to enjoy running after the ball almost as much or maybe a little more than trying to catch it. When they finished playing, Doris threw the ball back where she'd found it and then they walked around looking at other buildings and enjoying how big and spread out everything was.

Before long the loud bell clanged again, with the same response. Home kids came from every direction, and streamed into the dining room once more. Just as they did at lunch, Os sat with his team and Mary sat, without speaking at all, in the seat where Os would have been. Nancy and Christine did everything together. Doris hoped that soon she would find a friend, too, but for now, she still had Alert to watch over.

Chapter 22
The Creek

$\mathcal{W}$ith everyone seated, Father Nelson came into the dining room for announcements and the blessing.

"Good evening, children," he started. "I hope you have all gotten settled into your bunks, and are starting to feel at home here." Os looked at Doris. His eyes widened, and his expression told her that something was very wrong. When Father Nelson spoke of settling in a bunk, Os realized that he had been so busy playing that he hadn't even thought of where he would sleep. Doris watched as Bruce tapped Os on the shoulder and whispered something right into his ear. Whatever he said, Os's expression completely relaxed, and he and Doris could again focus on Father Nelson's announcements.

"Most of you have been here many times, and know what to expect from day to day, but for those children who haven't been here before, tomorrow is still bath day, but since we don't have any bath tubs here, everyone will bring a cake of soap[4] and shampoo down to the creek. Each

---

4 Procter Gamble made bars of soap called Large Size Twin Cake Ivory Soap. This soap floated. This would have been important

person will bathe in his or her bathing suit. If you don't have a bathing suit yet, see Miss Bersager after dinner."

Father Nelson continued, "there are fewer Saturday chores, and they are spread around, so they won't take as long. There will be a list in each cabin, telling what each of you is expected to do. Until we know who is in which bunk, Miss Bersager will hand out clean clothes to the girls, Miss Johnson to the boys and Miss Flotten to the Tots. Since all the bunks have clean sheets today, starting next Saturday, you will each be given a clean sheet, just like in Fort Lee. Each of you is to change your bed and bring the used sheet and your last week's clothes down to the laundry building. For the new children, the laundry room is right next to this building, under the room that the Tots sleep in.

The older boys will take turns pumping water to fill the tanks for the laundry and the kitchen. I don't think there are any new big boys, this year. We might have a few more boys coming to spend the summer with us later on, and if they do, they will be expected to help with the pumping, as well. Does anyone have any questions?"

Doris wanted to ask what a pump is and why don't the girls get to do it, but she decided to wait and find out on her own. It didn't sound like fun to take a bath in a bathing suit, but she didn't especially like taking her bath with two other girls in the tub at the same time, in Fort Lee, either. She still did not know what a creek was - or where it was, but she decided that she would probably be laughed at if she asked those questions now, so she decided to wait and see about that, as well.

"Okay," said Father Nelson, "if no one has any questions, let's pray. Heavenly Father, thank you for the beautiful weather we have had on this first afternoon here. We ask your blessing on our food, and that you would bless us to your service. In Jesus's name, Amen."

The Creek

After dinner, Os made his way through the chairs and children, and told Doris that Bruce said there was a lower bunk in their room, for him. "Bruce said that since I'm five, I'm allowed to be in the boys's room, instead of with the Tots. I left my box on your bed. I'll pick it up when I get my bathing suit." Doris was happy for Os's promotion. She didn't mention it to Os, but she was concerned that Alert would miss having him in the same room with him.

Doris brought Alert to the Tots's room right after dinner, to help him get settled for bed. She hoped he would be more comfortable in his new room if they spent a little extra time there together.

Miss Flotten was busy making up the little bunks and cribs. Most of the Tots were outside playing, with two of the older girls watching over them. "Miss Flotten, can I still come to take care of Alert early in the morning?" Doris asked.

"Well, Dukken, there are two girls who will be helping me with the Tots all summer. They should be able to help with Alert, too. I was thinking that it might be easier for Alert to adjust to this change, if you came to him, like you have been doing before school, for a week or so. As he gets used to the other girls, you can probably spend more time playing with children your own age. Most of the older children spend a good part of the day at the creek, and the Tots don't go there, because they can't walk that far. What do you think?"

Doris thought for a few seconds before she started to talk. She wished she could think a lot longer, but she didn't want to be rude. "I think that would be good. I will really miss seeing Alert in the morning. We both feel happy to start our day that way."

She really needed more information before she answered about time at the creek. "Miss Flotten, you said the children have to walk to the creek. Is it very far?"

"I guess it's about a mile. That would be like walking almost all the way to your school in Fort Lee," said Miss Flotten.

"And the Tots don't go there?" Doris asked.

"No, Dukken. The Tots don't know how to swim. Once in a while the older Tots are driven to the creek for a bath. There has to be one adult to hold and bathe each Tot. The younger Tots get washed in tubs in the laundry room, where the water is heated for them."

"Miss Flotten, I don't know how to swim either!" Doris said.

"Oh, you'll learn quickly. There are many places where the water is deep enough to learn how to swim, but not so deep that you wouldn't be able to just stand up and have your whole head well above the water."

"Will Christine and Nancy be able to go to the creek?"

"Probably not right away. Miss Bersager will have to be there with them until she is certain they will be able to be there safely by themselves. She doesn't have the time to go there every day."

Comfortable that Miss Flotten wouldn't laugh at her, Doris asked another question: "What is the pump, and why can't the girls take a turn to do that?" Doris asked.

"That's where we get all the water we use here. Deep under the ground, there is water. Someone has dug down to the water, and put in what's called a well. In the olden days a well used to be an open hole in the ground and people would put a pail on a rope and drop it into the well, then pull it up full of water. Then someone invented a pump. That's that black metal thing that looks like a fire hydrant when you first come through the archway. It has a long handle on the top. When someone pumps it up and down, it makes water come up from the well. Here it is set up to put that water into a big tank between the dining room and the laundry room, and that's where the water that comes out of the faucet comes from. It's pretty hard to pump it for a long time, so the boys take turns. The reason the girls don't do it, is - well - I guess someone decided that it is better for the boys to build up their muscles, rather than the girls. That's a good question."

Doris was glad Miss Flotten didn't tease her because she didn't know these things.

"Did you get your bathing suit, yet, Dukken?"

"No, not yet," Doris answered.

"I'll play with Alert for a while. Why don't you run and get one from Miss Bersager, before there aren't any left that fit you."

"Thanks, Miss Flotten, I'll do that right now. Will she be in the girls's building?"

"Yes, Dukken, and that building is called the farmhouse."

"Oh, thanks so much Miss Flotten, I'll be back in a little while to get Alert ready for bed."

Miss Bersager was in the farmhouse, talking with Christine, Nancy, and three other older girls. "Doris" she said, as Doris pulled open the screen door. "You're just in time. Do you know Mildred, Grace and Fanny?" You probably think they've been here forever, but they only came two months before you and your family. This is their first summer at camp, too, so I wanted to give you all bathing suits and caps, soap and shampoo and tell you about bath days at the creek. Girls, this is Doris. She is Christine's sister, and they have two younger brothers who came a month before the girls did."

"Hi Doris," the girls said, almost together. Then the oldest one, whom Doris had seen working in the kitchen said. "I have seen you helping your little brother in the dining room many times. He's so cute!"

"Thanks," said Doris. "We're all very happy to be together, at The Home."

"Okay, girls," said Miss Bersager getting back to business. "Doris, the others already have their suits and caps. I'll help you find one that fits you, after I explain about bathing in the creek."

Miss Bersager continued talking to all six new girls. "The first thing you'll notice is that the water is very cold. It might be uncomfortable at first, but after a while, you really will get used to it. Most days will just be fun and when it gets real hot out, you'll be glad the water is cold. Next thing is that the water in the creek is always moving, going in the same direction. Sometime, while you're at the creek on Saturdays, find a spot down creek, that means where the water has already gone past the other kids. Reach in under your suit and wash your personal places with the soap you've brought with you, and as the water flows around you, wash the soap off. To wash your hair, dunk your head under the water to get your hair wet and use your shampoo. Make sure to get a nice big lather all over your head, and then dunk under the water again and run your hands through your hair, as the water takes the suds down creek. When your hair feels nice and squeaky clean, you're finished! It's best to let your soap dry on a rock, then you can carry it back in your bathing cap."

This did not sound very appealing to Doris. *Water that is cold - no* very *cold. Water that isn't in a bathtub, but runs past you and carries your soapsuds down creek, wherever that is?*

None of the other girls seemed too concerned about any part of the instructions, so Doris decided she would wait until she actually saw for herself what this creek was really like, before she decided whether she would like or hate it.

"Doris, here are two suits. Try them on and see which one is most comfortable. See that building with the little wooden cross on top, right next to the laundry? That is the chapel. Upstairs from the chapel is the nurse's room, and there is a changing room there, where all the girls go to get their bathing suits on. Since tomorrow will be the first time any of you will go to the creek, I will go with you after lunch. It should be a little warmer by then. Put your bathing suits and shoes on, and bring your bathing caps, soap, shampoo and a towel, and meet me by the bell. We'll walk to the creek together."

With that, Doris carried the two bathing suits over to the chapel and tried them on. She had never worn a bathing suit, and it felt very strange to her. Both of them came down almost to her knees, so she decided that must be the way it was supposed to be. There was a little more room to move in one, so she chose that one and brought the one that was a little tight, back to Miss Bersager.

Alert was mostly ready for bed when Doris returned. She sat with him, as she did in Fort Lee, until he was almost asleep, then she put him into his crib. He laid himself down and put his thumb into his mouth while Doris put a light blanket over him.

It still wasn't very dark out, but it was definitely bedtime, and Doris was ready for the day to come to an end. It felt a little strange, but a lot good, to have her own bed, for the first time in her life. The new bed was a thin mattress lying on top of a board that was held by poles at every corner that went from the floor to the ceiling, and gave the support for Christine's bed, below her, too. She had a sheet that went on top of the mattress then folded back and covered her, as well. She also had a little blanket that she kept beside her in case she got cold during the night. Doris took a few minutes to unpack her box. There was a board that was sticking out from the wall up near her head where she placed her mother's picture, the paper with Pappa's address on it, the shoe box with her doll and its clothes and the toy her father had made her, and her little pile of clothes. It was fun to have her own little space to personalize. Once that was done, she settled herself into the sheet.

Everyone was in bed, but one by one, they all began to laugh. No one had been talking, but there was so much noise coming from outside the windows, that none of them could get to sleep.

One of the older girls finally explained. "That's the noise the crickets make. This is their favorite time to call to one another. You'll get used to it, soon. I like to think of it as a camp lullaby. It's nice to go to sleep with them singing to me. I actually miss them when we go back to Fort Lee after the summer."

As she lay there trying to imagine the cricket's calls as a lullaby, she heard a different sound. Christine was whispering up to her. "Doris, I can't get to sleep. I think I miss having you in my bed. Could you come down here, or could I come up to be with you?"

Doris felt a little selfish, but mostly she was tired. She thought for a few seconds, then said, "Christine, roll your little blanket up and put it right behind you, and make believe it's me." That must have helped, because after the rustling of blankets, there were no more sounds from the bed below her.

Doris didn't believe she could ever fall asleep with so much noise, but before she realized she had, the morning light was coming in through the windows. She sat straight up, hoping she wasn't too late to get Alert out of bed. Quickly, she pulled her clothes and socks and shoes on, and jumped down off her bed.

She made a quick trip to the outhouse before running down the hill to the big field, across the field, then up the other side to the Tots's room above the laundry. There he was - standing in the corner of his crib, looking lost. When he saw Doris, he smiled, and danced up and down with relief that he had not been left alone. His arms stretched out to greet Doris, and when she lifted him out of the crib, he held her more tightly and longer than usual.

Alert no longer wore diapers, so she knew he would need to use the potty they had set up in the corner for the Tots. After that she got him dressed, and put on a sweater, since the morning air felt cool. Then she scooped him up and brought him down the steps from the Tot's room, and they found a sunny spot to sit together and wait for breakfast.

While they were waiting, Doris asked him questions about who was sleeping in his room last night and the things they saw and did the day before. He happily answered the best he could, with every single word he had learned, and using his little finger to point at things he didn't have words for yet.

Saturday morning went quickly. Doris, Nancy and Christine were on the list to sweep the floor of the farmhouse and wash the steps coming into the room they slept in. The older girls showed them where the brooms, soap, scrub brush and pails were. Alert sat and played on Christine's bed while the girls worked around him.

After lunch Doris settled Alert in his crib for a nap, and Miss Bersager assured her that she would stay near him as he slept, in case he was frightened.

The girls met Miss Bersager at the bell outside the dining room. When all six girls, and Oscar were together, they started their walk. As they went through the big iron arch, Doris turned around and finished reading the sign she didn't get to finish when the bus pulled in. It said *"Christian Orphan Home for Children." Just like the sign on the pillar down by the main road in Fort Lee,* thought Doris.

Once they were through the arch, they turned right and walked, and walked and walked. Christine and Nancy started to lag behind, but Oscar was right up with the older kids and Miss Bersager. Every once in a while Miss Bersager would call back to the stragglers, "Come on, you two. We don't want to lose you."

There was nothing to look at as they walked, except lots and lots of trees on both sides of the road. They passed a field with trees all lined up in neat rows. Miss Bersager said that was an orchard where apples were grown, and she explained that once the apples were ready to be picked, the farmer would pay Home Kids to work for him. That would happen toward the end of the summer.

Although the scenery didn't change, the screams and laughter of children at play now filled the air, and the longer they walked, the louder the happy sounds got. They could also hear a loud, almost roaring sound that Doris didn't recognize. She would find out that it was made by the swiftly moving water pushing its way through the woods and around large rocks in the middle of its path.

They crossed a little wooden bridge, that had water rushing under it, went up a hill, then turned right onto a path that came off the road. The sound of water splashing and rushing and children playing became louder and louder, and through the trees, the reflection of the sun on the water looked like sparkles.

A short distance down a rocky, dirt path, there was a clearing where the sun managed to push a few of its rays through the trees. The ground was damp, bare dirt and there were several large rocks with colorful clothes draped over them. Shoes, mostly in pairs, which had been kicked off by the children who were already in the water, were spread like colored sprinkles over the clearing, and on the other side of the clearing, was *THE creek.*

The air smelled just like clean sheets when they came off the clothesline, only stronger. The darkness of the woods gave way to bright sunshine on the creek, causing the newcomers to squint, to adjust their eyes to the light.

So this is it, Doris thought. *Now I finally know what the creek looks like.* Other than when she was on a ferry, this was the closest she had been to this much water. It looked beautiful; clean, clear, and lively. The creek was about as wide as the road, and just like Miss Bersager said, the water was moving all in the same direction, splashing as it crashed into big boulders in the middle of the creek. She couldn't see where it started, but it was moving swiftly past them and disappearing around a bend after it passed the children. There were children of various sizes on each of three large rocks in the water and more kids in the water, swimming, talking, laughing, teasing and splashing each other. They continued their play, without any indication they had seen Miss Bersager arrive with her ducklings, ready for their first outing to wet their feathers.

None of the Hauklands had ever been in water to play, except when the horse drawn cart with the water tank, sprayed the cobblestone street they lived on, to keep the dust down and clean the horse manure off the street. They would play in the puddles it left at the curb, until they evaporated.

Doris noticed that right by the edge of the water was a little shallow pool where the water was hardly moving. *That would be a good place to start*, she thought. She had taken off her shoes, and she stepped right into the little pool. Her feet felt like she had set them on a big block of ice and she couldn't keep from jumping back out of the water. Miss Bersager and the others laughed at Doris's reaction.

"It's okay," Miss Bersager said, "You'll get used to it."

Oscar, who had spent many hours sitting out in the cold watching the hockey games, took the next turn. As soon as his feet hit the water, his expression changed from concern to complete pleasure. This was where he belonged. Since he didn't know how to swim, and he wasn't as tall as the others, he didn't venture too far from the shore, but he did go in to his waist. As the girls watched, Os began to bounce up and down in the water, and slap the surface with both hands sending a splash that went out in every direction.

Os made it look like so much fun that one after the other all of the girls went in, but they each took one baby step at a time, occasionally gasping, until they were covered by water almost to their necks. Even Doris ventured back in. Once she was covered to her shoulders, she called to Miss Bersager, "you were right, Miss Bersager. It's cold, but it also feels good!"

Miss Bersager held Christine in a way that made her stay just above the water, with her head out of the water and her feet close to the surface. Then she said, "Christine, kick your feet - first one then the other, as fast as you can."

Christine did this so hard that there were big white bubbles in the water around her feet, and the splashes went way over Miss Bersager's head.

"Okay, now make little cups with your hands, and scoop the water out in front of you and pull it back to you." Christine seemed to understand perfectly, and she worked hard to do as she was told. "Now do both things together."

Christine put it all together and for a few seconds, Miss Bersager was able to pull her hands out from under her. She was able to keep her head above the water, all by herself. She soon began to slip a little further down into the water, so Miss Bersager held her up, while Christine caught her breath.

"That was fun, Miss Bersager, can we do it again?" Christine asked.

"Sure. Take a little time to rest, and then we'll try it again. Next time you come, you can find a spot where you can stand on your own, and keep trying this until you can swim."

Doris and Oscar had been carefully watching what Miss Bersager and Christine were doing. Doris asked Os, "Do you want me to hold you up?"

"No thanks," he answered. "I can practice it on my own."

Doris watched as time after time he tried and sunk until he was able to stay up for a few seconds, then longer and longer.

Miss Bersager, seeing how much the Hauklands were enjoying the water, decided that she would work with them every day, until they were all able to swim well enough to be at the creek with all the other children.

Doris found the bathing part a little uncomfortable, but it was okay and it really felt good and refreshing to have squeaky-clean hair. She quickly combed it with her fingers and fastened it with her elastics, so it wouldn't stick out in every direction.

There were two more things the Hauklands would quickly learn about the creek. When they got out of the water, there was something between several of their toes. It didn't hurt, but it felt weird.

"Miss Bersager, what is this between my toes?"

"Those are leaches, dear. You just have to pick them out then squash them between two rocks."

"OH! They're BUGS?" the children squirmed and squealed.

"Yes, but they're not harmful. Sometimes Doctors even put them on some of their patients to help them get better."

"I HATE them!" Christine screamed.

"You'll get used to them Christine. Soon they won't seem quite so bad. There's another thing I need to tell you. Sometimes while you're in the water, you will see a snake swimming past you. You don't need to be afraid; he has no interest in you. You just happen to be standing, or swimming where he's used to being when you're not here. As long as you don't bother with him, he'll just swim right past you."

"Is it a poisonous snake, Miss Bersager?" Oscar asked.

"Yes, Oscar, they are Water Moccasins, and they are poisonous, but Home Kids have been swimming here with them for years, and no one has ever been bitten. Just let them swim past you - don't try to catch them."

Not totally convinced that this creek thing was worth dealing with - the ice cold water, the leeches and the poisonous snakes, they decided they'd head back to the camp, and think hard about whether they'd like to return tomorrow for more swimming lessons.

The next day was very hot and after running and playing all morning, when Miss Bersager asked if they were ready for another swimming lesson at the creek, they welcomed the thought of that icy cold water.

Chapter 23
A Friend for Doris

The routines at camp were very easy to settle into. It seemed like, except for Saturday morning when there were specific chores to be done and Sunday when there was Chapel to attend, the only things that they had to do were show up in the dining room every time the bell rang, and be in their bunk houses shortly after the bell rang in the evening, for devotions and to go to bed.

At first, it was hard for Doris to leave Alert when they went to the creek. But most of the time they were at the creek, Alert was napping anyway. Doris had also noticed that more and more, Alert looked happy playing with the other Tots and the older girls who were helping Miss Flotten during the summer.

With Alert, Oscar and Christine finding other friends their age to play with, Doris was able to finally spend a little time with children her own age, and do the things that girls who are almost nine years old like to do. She had met Mary in the dining room. She didn't talk much, but she did say she liked to play ball, jump rope, and go swimming. Doris hoped that some day they would do some exploring in the woods, and go to the creek together.

Mary had been in the Home for many years. When school ended, Mary's best friend, Ruth, who had also lived at the Home for many years, went to live with her Aunt somewhere in Pennsylvania. Mary was lost without Ruth, and since they had been in West Park, she spent all day, every day, in the farmhouse.

Doris tried to get her to come out to jump rope, or take a walk, but she always said, "No, I'd rather just stay here and think about Ruth."

Doris knew this wasn't healthy, and she also knew she wanted to make new friends. She didn't know if she would ever be able to get Mary out of the farmhouse, except for meals, but she was willing to try anything to help Mary come out of the dark, lonely bunkhouse. Pappa had sent Doris five stamps and five envelopes after they arrived in West Park, so she could write to him, and he said he would send more, soon.

"Mary," she said, "I know you miss Ruth a lot. I bet she misses you, too. I'm going to sit outside under the tree and write a letter to my father. I have an extra notebook, and my father gave me five stamps and five envelopes. Why don't you come out with me and write to Ruth?"

"That wouldn't work," Mary said, glumly. "All I know is that she is somewhere in Pennsylvania. I don't have the address, and I don't even know her Aunt's name."

"I bet that if you wrote to Ruth, Father Nelson would know her Aunt's address, and he could send the letter for you," said Doris. "Maybe Ruth is just as sad and lonely as you are, and hearing from you would cheer her up."

"Do you think she might write back?" Mary asked Doris.

"It's worth trying. We could bring the letter to Father Nelson at lunch. If it gets to the post office this afternoon, and she writes back, you might get the letter in a week or two."

"It would be awful good to get a letter from Ruth," said Mary, "Let's go. I have a pencil in my bunk. I'll get it."

Doris and Mary sat in the shade of the fattest tree outside the farmhouse. They both leaned back against the rough bark, and drew their knees up to make a table to support the notebooks they wrote on.

"Thanks, Doris. This is fun."

They each started writing. Doris wrote:

Dear Pappa,

West Park is beautiful. The sky is so blue and the air is so fresh. There are more trees here than I have ever seen before. I am sitting under a big fat one with my new friend, Mary.

There are so many things to do here, and we are all making new friends. Oscar plays baseball with the older boys. They let him be a sort-of catcher.

He stands way behind the batter to run after balls that get past the batter and he also gets to stay way, way out in the field to run after balls that go further than usual. Everyone calls him Os now and his teammates treat him very well.

Christine and Nancy have made a few more friends, and they all play dolls, and ball and hide and seek.

Alert seems to be happy here, too. There are a few older girls who play with the Tots all day. Alert is talking more and learning new words each day. Miss Flotten says he seems to have a will of his own, and sometimes he just won't do what the others are doing, but most of the time when I see him, he is playing happily. He feeds himself, now, and except for Os, who sits with his team, the rest of us sit together during meals.

Guess what, Pappa? Doris wrote, but Mary interrupted her.

"Doris, is it all right if I use another piece of paper?"

"Sure," Doris answered.

Then she continued her own letter.

Os, Christine and I can swim! Miss Bersager taught us all and watched us for a week before she told us we were all safe to swim on our own! It is so much fun. The water is cold, and when we finish swimming, we have to pick leeches out from between our toes. But we are getting used to that already.

Doris paused her writing and looked up. Mary was writing as fast as she had ever seen anyone write, and she was smiling! That was the first time Doris had seen Mary smile, since they came to West Park.

Doris continued her letter.

Pappa, if only you could come and see us here, it would really be perfect. I hope you are feeling better, and it will be easier for you to come to see us once we get back to Fort Lee.

I love you, Pappa.

Love, Doris

Doris folded her letter and carefully fit it into an envelope. She knew how to address the envelope and she placed the stamp upside down in the upper right corner. Her mother had told her that putting the stamp upside down meant that you loved the person you were sending the letter to.

Mary ended her letter and asked Doris for an envelope and stamp. Mary looked like a different girl to Doris. Even though the letter was finished and in an envelope, Mary was still smiling.

"Doris, do you think we could go find Father Nelson now, just in case he goes to the Post Office before lunch?" Mary asked.

"Sure - let's try!"

Doris put the remaining envelopes, stamps and her writing book back in her box on the shelf above her bunk. Then the two girls ran off to find Father Nelson.

They seemed to be just behind him. The first three places they stopped, someone told them he had just left there. His car was still parked next to the dining room, so they knew he hadn't gone to the post office, yet. The forth place they tried, the Chapel, was like finding gold at the end of a treasure hunt. There was Father Nelson, sitting quietly behind a large desk with lots of papers spread out in front of him. The desk was very worn, with scratches and dents on every surface, but Father Nelson still looked very important.

"Come in, young ladies," said Father Nelson. "What can I do for you?"

"Doris and I just wrote letters," Mary blurted out excitedly. "Mine is for Ruth. She used to be here, but she went to live with her Aunt. Do you know an address I could send this letter to?"

"Oh you mean Ruth Christiansen," said Father Nelson, "the girl who went to Pennsylvania with her Aunt."

"Yes," said Mary.

"Sure, I have her new address in the files. If you leave the letter here with me, I will fill out the address and bring it to the Post Office after lunch, today. Doris, do you need an address, too?"

"No thank you, Father Nelson. My letter is to my father, and I already have his address."

"Okay, girls, I will take your letters and get them both in the mail this afternoon."

Doris didn't know what to expect next. There was still enough time to play before lunch, but she expected Mary to head back to the farmhouse.

"Doris, would you like to take a hike in the woods? I have been there many times but not since we got here this year. I was wondering if there are any changes along the paths. Want to?"

Did she ever! This was Doris's dream. Since the day they had arrived she had wondered what was in the woods. "YES!" Doris answered. "Let's Go!"

They took a path that started at the opposite end of the field from the big gates they went through to get to the road. The path started out pretty wide, but after just a few feet, it became so narrow that Doris had to walk behind Mary. There were bushes down low - they had some little green balls on them. "What are those tiny green balls?" asked Doris.

"They're blueberries, Doris. They start out green, then in a few weeks, they get bigger and fatter, and start to turn blue. When they get real dark blue, we pick them. We can eat the ones we find in the woods. There is a farmer near here who grows blueberries on taller bushes. Sometimes he will pay us Home Kids to pick the berries for him to sell."

The bushes were pretty, with small, light green, oval leaves. Doris tried to imagine picking berries from a bush and eating them. She looked all around, taking in all the different bushes and trees. It was darker in the woods - only little rays of sun made their way through all the lush green leaves. In one section, there were mostly what Doris called Christmas trees. Mary corrected her, but in a nice way, without making fun of her. She said, "These are pine trees." Under the pine trees were a lot of thin, brown things that made the ground look like a rug and feel soft to walk on. The woods were even darker under the pine trees.

Next, they came to a spot where there were a lot of trees that had been cut. The sun was able to shine all the way down to the ground. Some of the logs from the cut trees were lying on the ground in piles, and some of them were made into a little hut. They were leaning into each other, and someone had tied them together at the top. Mary explained that this is where the boys like to play Cowboys and Indians. This is their teepee. They were both glad there weren't any boys there while they were hiking. The path continued on the other side of the clearing, but the girls only got a little further into the woods when they heard the bell, and they both knew they had to turn back for lunch.

"Thanks, Mary," said Doris. "I have wanted to do this ever since we got here."

"Thanks for helping me to write to Ruth, Doris. I hope I hear back from her, but even if I don't, when I was writing to her, it felt like I was with her, and it made me feel so much better."

Chapter 24
Nine Years Old

$\mathcal{P}$appa had sent several letters to West Park. The Haukland children all gathered together while Doris read his letters to them. He said he was feeling better, and he was happy living at Mrs. Boardsen's house. In his last letter, he said that he was going to send a package. Alert didn't seem to understand what that meant, but Christine, Oscar and Doris checked every day, at least twice to make sure it hadn't arrived while they were busy playing. Finally a big box wrapped in brown paper and addressed to Doris, Christine, Oscar and Alert Haukland arrived!

Doris and Christine had just returned from the creek, and saw the package first, but they had decided no one would open it until they were all together. Christine waited outside the dining room while Doris ran to get Alert. He was just waking up from his nap. The excitement in Doris's voice as she lifted him from his crib was contagious. Whatever was making Doris so happy was something Alert wanted in on. He ran right along with her, as fast as his little legs could carry him.

They headed back to the baseball field to get Os.

As soon as they were all together, Doris announced, "This is the package Pappa sent us." With that, all four began tearing pieces of brown paper off and throwing them into the air. It felt like a party. The box had four more boxes inside of it. Two had Happy Birthday written on them, and two had plain brown paper on them. When they took the first box out, it had *Oscar* written on it. Oscar's eyes widened as he began to strip the paper off. "WOW a baseball glove!" As soon as it was out of the box, it was on his hand, and he was punching his opposite fist into its pocket. "Wow," he said again grinning from ear to ear. The next package was also wrapped in brown paper. It was labeled *Christine*.

Christine smiled broadly as she took her package and settled on the ground to open it. "What is this Doris?" she asked, holding up the package so Doris could read the words, and explain it to her.

"Water wings," Doris read. Turning the box over, they saw a picture of a woman swimming with what looked like two flattened bags of air attached to a band around her waist keeping her up at the top of the water. Under the picture, it said "Learn to Swim by One Trial - Great Sport

in the Water." Christine looked a little disappointed. , "I already know how to swim," she said.

"That's good, Christine, but it looks like it helps you stay up in the water longer, so you can have even more fun while you're swimming and playing." said Doris.

"Okay" said Christine, "I'll try them tomorrow."

The next box had *Happy Birthday, Alert* written on it. Doris announced "this one is an early Birthday present for Alert. Pappa said Alert's birthday is next week." The others wanted to help Alert tear off the paper, but after watching Os and Christine, Alert now understood that this was *his* package, and he wanted to do it himself! He pushed their hands away and tore open his package. His eyes were wide and riveted on the box, his body racing to get the wrapping off before his curiosity made him explode.

Pappa knew Alert loved trucks. Alert reached into his box and with both hands, pulled out a bright yellow, beautifully carved wooden truck with wheels that spun around on a metal axle, and an open box in the back of the truck. Doris showed Alert that he could load the back with stones or grass, or sand and move it from place to place. Alert was no longer interested in anything else that might or might not be in the big box. He immediately leaned over with the truck between his legs. With his arms stretched out and positioned on the top of the cab, he pushed it along the ground. His lips vibrated rapidly as a spray of saliva accompanied the motor-like sound that poured out of his mouth.

"What did you get, Doris?" asked Oscar. "Is it your birthday?"

"Yes," Doris answered. Yesterday was my birthday.

Doris opened the last package, wrapped in brown paper with *Happy Birthday Doris* written across the top.

Inside the box there was a letter. It was from Pappa. Since this was her present, Doris read the letter silently.

Dear Doris,

You are now nine years old. I am so proud of you. I have sent you a jump rope, but you must look carefully in the box to find another tiny box. This was your mother's ring. It is very small and you will have to be careful that you don't lose it. You are a very responsible young lady, and I believe that your mother would want you to have this ring. I hope it will make you happy and will remind you of how much your mother loved you. Happy Birthday, my very grown up daughter.

"Happy Birthday," Oscar said.

"Happy Birthday," Christine said.

A little voice about 10 feet away said "Hoppy Borfday, Sissa."

As Alert continued to play with his truck, the others gathered up the scraps of paper and they put all the trash in the big pail, to be burned. Os returned to the baseball field punching his fist into his new glove. Christine went back to the farmhouse, changed into her play clothes, and ran back out to meet up with Nancy and some of their new friends. Alert joined the other Tots, where he continued to play with his truck for the rest of the afternoon.

Doris went to the farmhouse. Since her bathing suit was already dry, she climbed up into her bunk, before changing into her play clothes, to savor her birthday celebration. She re-read Pappa's letter, then opened one little box that contained a jump rope and a smaller box that was the little case that held her mother's ring.

She took the picture her father had brought to her in Fort Lee, and looked closely to see if her mother had the ring on, when the picture was taken. She couldn't really see it, but she decided she would pretend it was there, but just hidden in the folds of her mother's dress. She slipped the ring onto each of her fingers, but it wouldn't stay on any of them, not even her thumb. Doris decided she would tie a string through it, and hang it on a nail sticking out of the wall, next to her mother's picture, and just look at it now and then. Someday when it fit her, she would wear it.

She strained to remember her mother. She could remember sitting with her while they knitted and singing songs with her as they walked home from the nursing home, and her mother's gentle guidance as they prepared dinner for the family. The memories were pleasant and she was happy to have them.

She did not cry. She did not feel sorry for herself that, she was the only one who knew that yesterday was her birthday until the package arrived. For a brief moment, Doris allowed herself to wonder what it would be like if her mother was still alive. Then, without being told what to do or think, she gathered her thoughts into a prayer. "Father in Heaven, tell my mother that I will always love her. Tell her that we are all together and that we are very happy here. Pappa is living at Mrs. Boardsen's house, and he is okay, too. Tell her that I have my own bed now, with my own little shelf, and I will try hard not to lose her ring. Tell her that there are a lot of other children who don't have parents to take care of them either, so we all help each other. We each have special friends, but we are all called Home Kids. We are like a very big, happy family, and our mother's little family fits in real nice with all the other children. Thank you Heavenly Father that you are always with us, wherever we are."

The door to the farmhouse flew open and Mary called to Doris. "Doris! I just got a letter from Ruth! She said she was sad and my letter made her feel better. She told me all about her cousins and what they do each day. She says she is getting more comfortable there. Can you come out and play?"

"Just a minute, Mary. I need to get out of my bathing suit and get my play clothes on. I got a new jump rope. Can we try it out?"

Doris reading the first manuscript of Rooted

She was 97 years old.